THE LONESOME DEATH OF JOE SAVAGE

Family duty leads Tracy Keyes to search for his cousin, the notorious Wyoming bad man Joe Savage. Tracy hasn't seen Savage since they were boys, and isn't sure he'd even recognize his criminal cousin if they met. Being related to the infamous Savage makes things no easier for him, nor do the bounty hunters who dog his trail, believing that Tracy can lead them to the outlaw. By the end of the long journey, Tracy is convinced that he is only following Joe Savage into his own grave . . .

C. J. SOMMERS

THE LONESOME DEATH OF JOE SAVAGE

Complete and Unabridged

LINFORD
Leicester

First published in Great Britain in 2012 by
Robert Hale Limited
London

First Linford Edition
published 2014
by arrangement with
Robert Hale Limited
London

A catalogue record for this book is available
from the British Library.

ISBN 978–1–4448–2105–5

Published by
F. A. Thorpe (Publishing)
Anstey, Leicestershire

Set by Words & Graphics Ltd.
Anstey, Leicestershire
Printed and bound in Great Britain by
T. J. International Ltd., Padstow, Cornwall

This book is printed on acid-free paper

1

It seemed like there must be a thousand miles of travel ahead of him. He knew there were a thousand behind him. Wyoming was a long, long way from Waco, Texas. Tracy Keyes had started this journey as a trail-hand with the Double M outfit out of Waco. After forty-five days through the heat and dust and stink of the cattle drive he had reached Abilene to find a telegram waiting for him.

His mother had sent it the week before, not knowing how long he would be on the trail. Her sister, Enora Savage, had learned that her only son, Joe, had been cut down on his ranch in Wyoming, and had begged Tracy to look into matters. Both his mother and Aunt Enora were Eastern ladies and had no real idea of how large the West was, how far Kansas was from Wyoming.

Tracy considered ignoring the request. It would be easy to say the wire had not reached him. But the last line of the telegram sealed his decision.

'Please, son, do this for me. I know how I would feel if you were lost out in the wilds. Mother.'

It seemed that he might as well, considering that the other option was to ride back to the Double M and resume his repetitious duties as a ranch-hand. He had been paid; he had a good horse. He had never seen Wyoming, and figured he might as well take a look at it. He tried to rope a few of his friends into riding with him, but they were busy trying to see how fast they could spend their earnings in Abilene. The only one who considered accompanying him was a narrow man named Clive Tillit, who ultimately declined with the advice, 'Buy yourself a heavy coat, Tracy. I know it's the middle of summer, but it won't be when you get there, and Wyoming winters are nothing to be dismissed.'

Tracy took Tillit's advice and bought a buffalo coat, which he tied behind his saddle on this ninety-degree day. The dry-goods clerk seemed surprised but pleased with the sale. Outside, the sky was clear, sun-bright. Not wishing to take the chance of being stranded afoot on the plains if something should happen to Thunder, his big sorrel with stockings on his front legs, he purchased a little white mare named Changa to take along. Changa could also be used to carry his supplies. The mild-mannered little horse was one of Double M's remuda spares and so he was able to purchase it for a very reasonable price.

Early the following morning while the town lay sleeping and an eerie ground fog blanketed the grassland, Tracy struck out northward. There was a strange sort of pleasure in riding into the unknown with no real objective in mind, equipped for weeks of travel, a man alone on the plains. By mid-morning the fog had cleared away, defeated by the risen sun.

Tracy rode on, the flat prairie stretching out endlessly. He passed three or four tiny settlements, but stayed clear of them. He was in need of nothing. He saw a sod-buster already at work in his fields, guiding his plow behind his mule, and raised a hand. The farmer removed his straw hat and waved back.

As he rode, Tracy tried to recall what he knew of his cousin, Joe Savage. It was little enough. His Aunt Enora's only son, only child, Joe would have been about Tracy's age — twenty-seven, by now. They had not lived near each other, and Tracy could only recall visiting his cousin, playing with him, once. They must have both been around ten years of age then. It was said that they looked alike, but Tracy had no idea if they did or not — he could not remember his cousin's face. He could only recall that one day when the play had gotten rough and Tracy had been pinned face-up on the ground, his cousin kneeling on him, an upraised rock in his hand, a look of evil intent in his eyes. His mother and Enora had broken up the squabble before anything serious could happen, but Tracy avoided his cousin the rest of that afternoon.

So was that what had caused Joe's troubles? Had he remained violent, gone wild once he drifted into the western lands? Not having known Joe Savage as an adult, Tracy could only speculate.

The weather held hot and dry in the daytime; cool at night. Tracy did not press the horses, but allowed them frequent rests and pauses for water at any source they happened to come across. In two days he had not seen another living human being on the plains. He guessed that he was near to Nebraska now, or more likely northern Colorado, since he could see the massive bulk of the purple Rocky Mountains to the west.

There was a lot of game to be had if a

man was hunting — pronghorn antelope, a few buffalo and mule deer — but Tracy was not in the mood to take the time and trouble of killing, skinning, and butchering animals when he was well-stocked with beans and other essentials.

The fourth morning he rose from his bed, stretching the kinks out of his back. The morning was cooler than expected, the ground harder. Although he had been happy enough to ride alone after the commotion of the trail drive and the clamor of the town, he was starting to wish for the sight of another human face. He supposed that was human nature.

It was on the following morning after another chill night on the plains that he spotted the settlement ahead of him, lying next to a nameless river. The road he followed now was well-traveled, wide. There were the signs of many horses having been ridden this way, and some wagon wheel ruts. Wherever he was, it was a well-traveled route that he had intersected. It suited him. He could find a bed or even a haystack to sleep in this night, and something to eat besides his own rough trail cooking.

As he approached and entered the small, squat town he began to see the name 'Baker' on almost every business, so he assumed that was the name of the town. He had never heard of it, but then he knew almost nothing about Wyoming. He had heard of Cheyenne and Laramie, but that was the extent of his knowledge of the territory.

Tracy swung down from his sorrel in front of the Baker Stable, and led both ponies inside, aware of the trail-weary tightness in his thighs. He had traveled a lot of miles clamping a saddle between his legs, and they were letting him know that they had taken enough.

'Who's that?' a voice called querulously from the shadows of the hay- and animal-smelling barn.

'Just a traveler. I need to put up my horses,' Tracy called back at the shadows. That brought the response of a few grumbled swear words as if the man was unhappy with his own choice of occupation on this day. After a minute a man with a pitchfork in his hand, his face lined with deep furrows, came forward. He wore a red shirt under blue coveralls and scowled heavily by way of greeting. He grabbed Thunder's bridle nearly out of Tracy's hand and studied the sorrel's flank.

'I don't recognize that brand,' he said, squinting at Tracy Keyes. He switched his eyes to Changa who wore the same Double M brand and scowled still more deeply.

'I'd be surprised if you did — that's a Texas brand,' Tracy told him.

'Odd the way the letters are connected.'

'That's the way old Justin Mills designed it,' Tracy said. The stableman still had him fixed with a mistrustful squint.

'You ain't a horse thief are you?' the old man asked.

Tracy half-smiled. He was getting

tired of the man's attitude. 'No. I've got the papers on them in my saddle-bags if you want me to dig them out.'

'Never mind — probably forged anyway.'

Tracy had had enough. 'Is there another stable in town?' he asked.

'None where you'll get better care of your horses,' the old man answered. 'You're a little touchy, aren't you?'

'I suppose so,' Tracy replied. 'I've been long on the trail.'

'Heading for Montana, are you?' the stablehand asked, loosening the cinches on Thunder's saddle.

'No. Why would you think so?'

'This time of the year the Texas cattle drives are winding down. Those Montana ranchers, a lot of them English lords and such, start putting advertisements in the Kansas newspapers, offering top wages for cowhands. To a lot of the boys it sounds good and when they reach the Montana lands in summer with the grass thick and green, it looks even better, and they hire on.

'The trouble is they ain't seen anything like a Montana blizzard in Texas. They tell me whole herds freeze off — thousands of beef. You ever try herding cattle in a blizzard? Come spring most of the cowboys pull their freight out of there. Someone said that those Montana ranches lose as many men as they do cattle as soon as the weather gets warm enough to ride away. They're always short of men.' The stablehand shrugged. 'That's why I asked you if you were heading farther north.'

'Don't Wyoming ranchers have the same problems?' Tracy asked. 'Winters here are almost as hard, aren't they?'

'They can be hard,' the stablehand agreed, 'but down here we don't run that many cattle. And we've got a little more common sense. Anybody would've told those Montana ranchers what they were getting into — anyone but the men who were selling the land and the cattle to them — by mail a lot of the times.'

'Anyway,' Tracy said, untying his goods from Changa's back, 'That's not why I'm up here.'

'No? Looking for somebody, are you?'

'Yes,' Tracy had to admit. He had to start asking around somewhere; he might as well tell this man. 'His name is Joe Savage. Ever heard of him?'

'No, I'm just a newborn,' the man answered, his eyes narrowing, his scowl deepening. ''course I heard of him.' His eyes brightened a little. 'So that's what you are. Another bounty hunter?'

'You see, it's like this . . . ' Tracy started to explain, but the old man cut him off as he slipped Thunder's bit and unbuckled the throat latch on his bridle.

'That at least is a respectable profession,' the stablehand said. 'Better than being a cowboy by far. If your sort can rid the territory of men like Joe Savage, it will be a better place for all of us to live.'

'You did know him, then?'

'I know things he's done. They say he's dead, but I never seen the body. If you need any details about Savage, I recommend you talk to the town marshal just up the street there,' he said, motioning with his whiskered chin.

'Good luck to you, stranger,' the old man said. 'But I got to tell you that you're not the only man chasing that bounty. The last one beat you up here by just a few days.'

'But if Joe Savage is dead already . . .'

'That's what they're saying, but even if he is, you know how long it takes for the word to spread. A man who's been on the trail for weeks just getting here wouldn't necessarily know that. Besides, I'm not so sure Joe Savage is dead.'

'Can you tell me . . . ?'

'I already gave you my best advice, mister: go talk to the marshal. Me, I've got work to attend to.'

Thunder and Changa were led away into the stable depths and Tracy turned and went out into the day.

The sky was a clear, clean blue, unmarred by a single wisp of cloud. The town of Baker was bustling, but there was none of that urgent, almost frenetic, movement that you saw in a place like Abilene. Folks here knew where they were going, knew that they could make it without giving themselves a stroke, it seemed.

Pedestrians moved at a reasonable pace along the plankwalks; horses were held to a trot. No one gave Tracy more than a glance. Probably they all assumed that he was as the man at the stable had sized him up — a cowboy moving on toward Montana where the wages were high and the winter risks higher.

The stablehand had undoubtedly given Tracy the best advice: talk to the local lawman. He was beginning to get an idea about why Joe Savage had been killed, but he hated the idea of having to tell his mother and Aunt Enora that Joe had been an outlaw. It could be that there was another side to the story. If not, at the very least, he could visit Joe Savage's grave, though he couldn't see how that would comfort his aunt.

If there was a grave. If Joe Savage was really dead. The stablehand seemed unconvinced. The town marshal would certainly know more about it. For example, even if he had no knowledge of the manner of Joe's passing, he would certainly have received a bulletin canceling the bounty on him. That money, if claimed in Baker, would have to come out of the town's coffers until it could be reimbursed by the county or the territory — a slow process.

Thinking of the bounty caused Tracy to remember that he had been told that a bounty hunter had drifted into Baker only a few days earlier. True, news traveled slowly out in the West, but bounty hunters, successful ones at least, were not stupid. They constantly checked in with local law officers to see if a man they were after had had his bounty rescinded. That saved weeks, miles of trying to track down a man who had already been captured or had died.

All Tracy knew was that his cousin was supposed to be dead. The stable-man and a bounty hunter both seemed unconvinced. What did the marshal think?

Aaron Cutler was behind his desk, feet propped up, when Tracy entered the town marshal's office. Cutler was not an intimidating figure, but his eyes spoke of cold, deliberate efficiency. He looked to be of a certain type Tracy had encountered before. He would ask you once, pleasantly, to behave, and if you didn't comply, he would crack your skull for you.

'What now?' the marshal said without apparent malice.

'I'm looking for a man named — '

'Joe Savage,' the marshal finished for him. 'And I'll tell you what I told your friend: I don't have any idea where he is or what might have happened to him.'

'My friend?' Tracy asked, puzzled.

'Whatever he is. The other bounty

hunter. I haven't seen Joe Savage in three months, thank God. And I don't care if I never see him again.'

Tracy took a seat in a wooden straight-backed chair without having been invited. 'A rough man, was he?'

'Pretty rough,' the marshal said, his eyes narrowing. 'I mean, he didn't strike you that way, just as a pretty lively sort of man with an easy smile, but he sure managed to get himself into a lot of trouble.'

'In Baker, you mean?'

'No.' Cutler shook his head. 'We don't stand for that sort of stuff around here. The boys would have taken him out and strung him up. Worst I can remember is him getting into a fist-fight over at the Tip Top Saloon. But word came in from all over about him.

'I would guess that he saved Baker as a sort of safe haven where he could come and purchase his goods without trouble.'

'Is he dead?' Tracy blurted out.

'Some say he is, others say he isn't.

Me, I don't know and don't much care.'

'What's the county sheriff say?'

'We haven't got one,' Cutler said. 'They call this Johnson County, but as of now it hasn't been properly surveyed or mapped. It may be a part of Johnson County or may not. No one knows. All I know is this: when you ride into town from the south there's a sign identifying this as Baker — if the sign's still standing; if you come in from the north there's another sign that identifies the town as Baker. What happens between those two signs is my business; anything beyond them is not.'

'Where would you guess Savage has gone to?'

'That's the same question the last man asked me,' the marshal said. 'That thousand dollars on Joe Savage's head gets your sort all worked up, doesn't it?' Cutler looked thoughtful briefly. 'Well I guess it would — that's nearly three years of a cowhand's pay, isn't it?'

'Close to it,' Tracy agreed. He was

still watching Cutler expectantly. Finally the marshal leaned forward and looked directly into Tracy Keyes's eyes.

'I might as well tell you — I told the other bounty hunter: if I had to hazard a guess, I'd say that Joe Savage is still up around the Eagle Rock area. That was the last place we had him reported. That's where he might be.'

'If he's still alive.'

'If he's still alive,' Marshal Cutler said, nodding.

2

There was little point in pressing the marshal any further. Tracy decided that he needed some directions. He didn't know if Eagle Rock was nearby or a hundred miles away. He thought it must be fairly close if, as the marshal had said, Joe Savage had come into Baker for supplies when he needed them.

In need of information, Tracy ambled off toward the nearest saloon, which turned out to be the Tip Top, as Cutler had mentioned.

He didn't make it that far before he was pulled up short, rudely, by a man with a black mustache wearing a white shirt and faded yellow vest. The man stepped in front of him on the street and said roughly:

'Your horses are in the other direction.' The stranger had a lisp and one bad eye, which was clouded.

'I guess I know that,' Tracy replied softly.

'Here's something else you should know,' the man said in a low growl. 'I don't like anybody dogging my back-trail. Get it?'

'I've nothing to do with you,' Tracy answered. The stranger was starting to irritate him.

'No? You're looking for someone, right? Joe Savage? They told me at the stable. And I saw you come out of the marshal's office just now. The name is Jack Warren, and Joe Savage is my meat, sonny. I'll brook no interference.'

'Joe Savage is dead,' Tracy said.

'So some say. Me, I doubt it, and as you know there's a thousand dollars on his head. There's no other reason you should be looking for him, is there?'

Yes, there was, but Tracy didn't feel the need to stand in the middle of the street in a strange town, discussing it with a man he didn't know. 'I'm not trying to interfere with you,' he replied.

'See that you don't,' the mustached man warned before he turned away and walked across the street.

No, Tracy wasn't trying to interfere with the bounty hunter, but what was his obligation if it turned out that Joe Savage was actually alive? To Mother and Aunt Enora? Would they expect him to stand with his cousin in a fight? A cousin he had never loved and barely remembered.

And who was likely a thief and a murderer.

Wriggling his way into the Tip Top Saloon where the doorway was crowded with indecisive men trying to find a table, Tracy crossed to the bar and stood watching the plank wall behind the counter while he waited to catch the barman's attention. He was grateful that the place didn't have a mirror behind the bar as some places he had seen in Abilene and elsewhere did. Why anyone thought that a bunch of trail-dusty drunken men would want to look at themselves was a mystery to him. True, it kept someone from slipping up behind you unseen, but no one had any reason to wish to see Tracy in this unfamiliar country, in a town he had never been in before. Except the bounty hunter, Jack Warren, of course, and he had already given Tracy his warning. What Tracy wanted now was to find someone who knew the area. He had to get to Eagle Rock and see what could be learned there.

A lean man with a patchy beard, wearing a faded flannel shirt, eased up beside him at the bar and hollered to the bartender. He glanced once at Tracy, but then turned his full attention to the mug of beer that was delivered to him, downing it in heavy gulps. He immediately called for another. Tracy said nothing as the man finished the second mug, drying the trail dust or settling his nerves, whichever had him in such a hurry to down the brew in front of him.

When the second mug was emptied and the man had run his shirt cuff across his mouth, looking around hopefully, Tracy asked:

'Buy you another one, friend?'

The man had brown, hawkish eyes flanking a narrow nose. When he smiled it was not attractive, but it was nice to see the friendly response, broken teeth or not. 'Why, I wouldn't mind,' he answered and Tracy signaled the bartender for a fresh mug. He still hadn't finished his own. It was green and tasted a little like sawdust. It was almost cool. The man beside him received his new mug and hoisted it in a gesture of thanks.

'You're new in town,' his drinking partner said, looking Tracy up and down.

'Just passing through, really,' Tracy told him.

'On your way to Montana?' the stranger asked. Tracy was getting used to being taken for a drifting cowboy. He nodded without answering. He didn't want to start that whole conversation up again. Instead he told the man:

'I'm looking for someone who can tell me how to get to Eagle Rock.'

'Never been there myself, but my pal lived out that way for quite a while. Pete Beck is his name.' The drinking man was thoughtfully, hopefully, turning his empty mug in circles on the bar counter. Tracy again signaled the bartender.

'So where is Pete? In town now, is he?'

'Yeah. He'll be in any minute. He just went outside to throw up. Pete's got a weak stomach, but it's never kept him away from the whiskey.'

After a while Tracy began to wonder if the man, Pete, had given it up as a bad project, passed out, or possibly been arrested, but then a stumbling man with a stained shirt staggered their way and Pete grabbed on to the bar as if he had to or go down to the floor. His face was waxy, his eyes red as radishes.

'I need a drink. Real bad,' Pete said.

'I'm tapped out,' the other drinking man said. 'This friend of mine has been standing for me.'

The red eyes turned imploringly to Tracy who nodded his assent. It was not his business to decide whether the man should have another whiskey or not; it *was* his business to try to find his way to Eagle Rock.

Since neither of his two new acquaintances was all that steady on his feet, Tracy suggested a table, one of which stood unoccupied in the back corner near a window. With some effort, Pete almost dangling between them, they made their way there.

'Thanks, mister,' Pete said, wiping his lips after his second whiskey.

'It's all right.' Tracy leaned forward in his chair and clasped hands on the table. 'Look, I'm trying to get to Eagle Rock. I understand you know the area.'

'Know it! I practically built it. You can ask anybody up there what Pete Beck did for that town.' There was indignation building in Pete's voice. Before he could get started on the story of his life, Tracy repeated:

'I just need to know how to find the place.'

'Forty miles east. Do you know the Standish cutoff?'

'I don't know a thing about the country up here,' Tracy answered.

'Past Mirror Lake,' Pete nodded. His voice was growing progressively slurred, hard to understand. 'Wait — I'll draw you a map.' From the table beside them Pete snagged a cribbage pad and a pencil someone had left behind.

His map, surprisingly, was neatly drawn, not the chicken scratch Tracy had been expecting. Perhaps Pete had been a man of some talent in earlier years. Just now he was decorating the map with stick pine trees where he thought they stood.

'That's fine, Pete, I appreciate it,' he said, slipping the page from the pad from Pete's fingers.

'Tell everyone I said hello,' Pete said as Tracy got to his feet. 'Town's gotten big now. Started building a school-house, even got a real preacher who's going around baptizing everyone and such. Eagle Rock ain't what it used to be. When I built it . . . ' Pete was still reminiscing about the old days when Tracy slipped two silver dollars on to the table. Not that he couldn't have spared a bit more, left over from his Double M pay, but that was enough to satisfy them for the moment. Staying in the company of drinking men was a quick way to empty your wallet. He had gotten what he had come for and it seemed that two dollars on top of whatever else he had already spent on them was fair compensation.

He stepped out into the sunny day beyond the Tip Top's door and looked up and down the street, his eye out for the man with the yellow vest and black mustache, Jack Warren. He hoped not to encounter the bounty hunter again, but thought he probably would. Especially if Warren had been thinking along the same lines as Tracy. He would have to proceed cautiously to Eagle Rock, he knew. Tracy didn't think that a man who killed for a living would be too troubled about leaving a lone unknown rider dead on the side of a wilderness trail.

★　★　★

For days Tracy had been dreaming about only a few things — a bath and a mattress to sleep on. He trudged on toward the large sign, painted in crimson flourishes, that read 'Hotel Baker'. The building didn't look all that fancy, but Tracy didn't need fancy; he needed a clean, peaceful place to sleep. There were still foxtails and assorted stickers in his clothing and probably in his hair. He hadn't a mirror to check that, and no comb to do anything about it. Some of the dirt and vegetable matter clinging to his dirty clothes had probably ridden all the way from Texas with him.

It was time to wash up and put his head down on a real pillow. Every few months a man likes to clean up a little.

He was as sleepy and hungry as a man can get, but Tracy decided to take care of a little personal business first. He managed to find a dry-goods store and purchase a new pair of blue jeans and a dark blue shirt. These he took along with him as he walked to the barber shop up the street. He took a bath in a big zinc tub in the yard behind the establishment, soaking long enough in the soapy hot water that he dozed off. Then, after toweling off, he dressed in his new clothes and allowed the barber to wash, curry and trim his hair, shave his whiskers and splash him with a little bay rum.

Paying the barber for his services, Tracy stepped out on to the street again, feeling like a new man. A new, hungry man. He stopped a man on the corner and asked where a good place to eat was. He was directed to a small, neat business named the Copper Kettle, a yellow building with wide front windows, and was shown to a round table in the back of the place.

Dinner was rare roast beef cut in half-inch-thick slices, corn muffins, and baked potatoes covered with rich, dark gravy. The meal was almost dizzying as it settled into his stomach after months of chuck wagon fare and his own poor camp cooking. Tracy was nearly staggering when he again crossed the street, heading toward the Hotel Baker.

He paid at the desk and was given the key to a small upstairs room with a window looking westward, toward the mountains. There was a bed, a blanket, a pillow. Tracy just managed to tug his boots off before he caved in from tiredness and from the weight of the heavy meal he had devoured, and dropped on to the bed. As his head hit the pillow he counted himself as one of the luckiest men on earth. Someone could get real spoiled in no time with what town life had to offer.

Tracy awoke with a start, thinking someone had failed to awaken him to ride night shift on the herd. Then he looked around him and realized where he had landed. The sky outside was a pale rose color with a rank of cottonwood trees standing in silhouette before it. Somewhere a covey of quail was making pleasant chittering sounds. Tracy stretched his arms, placed his hands behind his head and watched the window in the room brighten as the sun floated higher into the dawn sky.

It would have felt good to laze the day away, but Tracy knew he was not going to get any decent sleep. His body was telling him he had had enough of resting, no matter how pleasant it had been.

Rising, he went out of the hotel and found his way to the Copper Kettle. There was the good scent of fresh coffee in the air and a dozen or so local men sat at the small tables, eating breakfast. Tracy saw Marshal Aaron Cutler there, drinking a cup of coffee. He nodded to the lawman but got no response. It did not matter; Tracy figured this would be the last time he would ever see the man with the badge.

For breakfast Tracy had three fried eggs, biscuits with milk gravy, and a slice of ham. He definitely would get fat and spoiled if he ever became a town man. Of course, he had no skills to sell, no way to make his way in Baker or any other town. Finishing his second cup of coffee, he rose and strode out into the low glare of the new sun, walking toward the stable.

Thunder watched him eagerly, Changa with some apprehension as he entered the dark barn. Both looked well-curried, satisfied with their care. Tracy thought he understood the slight expression of uneasiness in the white mare's eyes. She had no desire to hit the trail again after traveling from Texas to Abilene and now all the way to Wyoming. Here she had finally found a place to rest, to be combed and have all the feed and water she could want.

'I feel the same way,' he told the little mare. 'All the same, we've got to travel on.'

Thunder seemed more eager to be going. He had lived long in the wild country, on brackish water and dry grass, but there was a love of the freedom the long land offered in his blood. Tracy thought he understood Thunder's eagerness to travel on as well. He patted the big sorrel's sleek neck and called out to the stableman who eventually appeared, sleepy-eyed and slouching, slipping one strap of his overalls up on a narrow shoulder.

'Ready to go, are you?' the man said.

'Yes. Not eager, but ready. This isn't a bad little town you have here.'

'We manage,' the stablehand said, unlatching Thunder's stall. The man switched his eyes quickly to Tracy. 'You are going to be able to pay this morning?' he asked.

'Yes.'

'Working at a job like mine . . . sometimes men arrive here with their pockets full, smiling and happy. The next morning they've drunk it all up or gambled it away.'

'What do you do then?'

'Tell them to suck eggs and walk over to get Marshal Cutler. Some of those boys don't leave easily.'

There were several comments Tracy could have made, but instead he just thrust his hand into the pocket of his new blue jeans and showed the stable-hand a ten-dollar gold piece. The thin man nodded and led Thunder to where Tracy's saddle rested over a partition.

Tracy busied himself re-packing his canvas bags full of supplies and positioning them on the doleful Changa's back across her pack saddle. He tied them down with practiced hands and then went to where Thunder stood trembling with something like eagerness. He checked the twin cinches of the Texas-rigged saddle the sorrel carried. The stablehand scowled as if that were an affront to his abilities. Tracy held up a hand.

'I know, but I'm the one who would lose his seat.'

The stableman nodded, grudgingly smiled, and led Tracy to the cramped, airless office where he made change for the gold piece. Fifteen minutes later, Tracy was out of Baker and riding free across the short-grass plains. The low sun was in his eyes and there was a wind starting to rise, which bent the sagebrush on the hills around him and flattened the buffalo grass under his horses' hoofs. Farther away pine tees stood, not in ranks but in scattered clusters like communing monks.

He was no more than five miles along the trail before he realized that he was being followed. The men were not stealthy in their pursuit, but rather, dogged. They did not try to close the gap between them, but followed along for hour after hour. When Tracy would stop for a few minutes to study the map that Pete Beck had drawn for him and compare it with the surrounding countryside, the two men on his backtrail would halt as well.

One of them, Tracy knew. Jack

Warren. Although the bounty hunter with the black mustache had shed his yellow vest, perhaps believing it provided too good a target on open ground, Tracy recognized him even at this distance. The other man, short and stocky, was no one he had ever seen before. Both rode bay horses, though the stubby man's mount was a pony with shorter legs and seemed to be hairier, perhaps prematurely growing its winter coat.

There was nothing to be done about them. Besides, with just a little guessing or asking around, they already knew that he was headed for Eagle Rock. Tracy thought that they were guessing — wrongly — that he had been given Joe Savage's location.

He knew that they were not going to give up.

And, anyway, Joe Savage was dead, wasn't he? That was the question that rode with Tracy Keyes as the ponies plodded on across the plains. Until he reached Eagle Rock and found out for sure, it was still a mystery.

Tracy removed his hat and wiped the perspiration that was trickling into his eyes. The breeze was cool, but the high-riding sun was still hot. Looking up at the hill slope to his right, Tracy saw sunlight glint off something bright concealed in the pines. A rifle barrel? While he was still pondering the question, he saw a puff of smoke rise through the trees and then heard the sharp crack of a Winchester rifle. He grabbed for his own rifle, but he was slower than the men following. Both Jack Warren and his stubby partner already had their rifles unsheathed and were returning fire. Two more rifle shots sounded from the pines, but then fell silent as the bounty hunter and his friend poured lead through the muzzles of their guns.

Tracy didn't hesitate any longer. He didn't know what the fight was about or who the intended victim was, but he felt like a target out there on the meadow. He heeled Thunder roughly, aiming the big horse and the panicked white mare toward the forest opposite the gunman's position.

Another shot rang out, and this one came much nearer to him, biting into the trunk of a pine tree. And it had been fired from behind his back. It seemed that Jack Warren was willing to cut down anyone he could settle his sights on.

3

It was cool among the pines. The sunlight barely penetrated the thatchwork of the blue-green branches overhead. And as Tracy slowed the horses after their scrambling rush up the hillside, all was still on the mountain slope. He could hear the chattering of squirrels, and the shifting of the tree boughs as the breeze worked its way through the forest, but there was nothing else to be heard. He drew up in a shallow depression and sat, just listening, but he could hear no horses on his backtrail. Maybe Jack Warren's temporary rage had subsided.

Tracy started on again, moving in the general direction of Eagle Rock. He took to the high ground, gradually working his way eastward. Now, below him, he could see the glitter of sunlight on water.

Mirror Lake? Judging from the map

Pete Beck had drawn, it had to be. But the water below was not one lake, but two almost abutting ponds. Of fair size, to be sure, but no one could rightly term this a lake. Nor could it lay claim to the description 'mirror'. With the wind ruffling the surface of the water, it glittered in a yellowish, muddy way, a dim and unstable reflector.

She sat on a square boulder at the edge of the ponds, her arms around her knees, looking out dreamily at the surrounding country. Tracy had come upon her suddenly, unexpectedly, as he emerged from the trees. Young, long-haired, she glanced up at him with innocent blue eyes and smiled.

'Hello,' she said, smoothing down her white skirt.

'Hello,' Tracy said a little warily. Why this young woman should cause him to feel uneasy, he could not have said. It was her sudden appearance in the wilderness, of course. Finding her when his thoughts were on other matters.

'Isn't the lake lovely at this time of

day?' she asked eagerly, her eyes wide. 'You should see it at sunset, all orange and red and purple.' Her voice was excited. If Mirror Lake was only two muddy ponds to Tracy, it obviously meant more than that to her.

Looking in the direction she was, he noticed the pine trees crowding the shore and the distant mountains. He supposed it was beautiful in its way. But it wasn't a lake. Thunder pricked his ears and shuffled his feet and Tracy glanced deeper into the trees to see a burnished little roan picketed among the pines. The girl's horse, obviously.

'Is this your land?' Tracy asked the young woman.

'For now,' she answered with an enigmatic smile.

'Oh? You're having trouble?'

'Nothing I'd care to discuss — it's very complicated and would take too long to tell.'

'All right,' Tracy answered, having no wish to invade the woman's privacy — or to get distracted from his single

41

purpose for being in this country.

'Don't you think this is a lovely site for a chapel?' As she asked this, she slipped down from the rock, again smoothing her white skirt.

'Is that the plan?' he asked.

'Oh, yes!' she said brightly. Then her smile fell away. 'There are a few difficulties.'

'There always are,' Tracy told her.

'I know that — that's what my uncle would say. Oh, excuse me!' she said as she approached Thunder. She looked genuinely embarrassed. 'My lack of manners! My name is Karin Cole.' She spelled her first name for him, stroked Thunder's neck and resumed her smile.

'Tracy Keyes,' he replied.

'My uncle, you see, is the Reverend Roger Cole. We have come here to settle. Actually,' she said, 'we came West with the intention of converting the heathen Indians, but they are nomads, so hard to gather, and we have discovered that there are at least as many white heathens out here in need of salvation.'

Tracy had been told back in Baker that there was a preacher in Eagle Rock going around baptizing everyone he could get to agree with having it done. So that was this man, Roger Cole. A civilizing influence, Pete Beck had called him, although he had spoken with little enthusiasm.

'I'm glad to have met you, Miss Cole,' he said, touching the brim of his hat, 'but I'm afraid I have to be getting on my way now. I'd like to be in Eagle Rock before dark. Could you direct me . . . or would you ride that way with me and show me the trail?'

'Oh, no, I wouldn't feel comfortable doing that,' she said, flushing a little. 'But you're headed in the right direction. Just over the knoll you'll find a trail that leads north for a little way and then forks. If you take the fork to the east it will lead you right into Eagle Rock.'

'I thank you,' Tracy said, 'and I wish

you good luck in solving whatever problems you are having with getting a chapel built out here.'

'And I wish you luck, Mister Keyes, in whatever enterprise it is that you have in mind.'

Eagle Rock was a neatly laid out little town although there wasn't much of it. The founders (Pete Beck among them?) had given the matter some consideration, rather than letting it grow in whatever sprawling way suited the newest builder as frequently was the case in newly settled country. The streets were laid out in a regular grid, though the buildings on some of them were widely spaced with weedy vacant lots between them. From the hill slope Tracy could also see four small patches of pine trees growing around town, perhaps left uncut to form town parks.

Eagle Rock was a neat-looking place, but situated where it was, it had little hope of ever growing much. Perhaps that was what the people living here wanted.

Descending in the shadows cast by the hill and deepened by the pine forest, Tracy reached the town at the hour before sunset. The western sky was already a muddy red, streaked with deep purple. The wind had not increased, but it had definitely grown cooler. Eagle Rock seemed destined for a short summer and long following winter.

The lanterns in town were slowly being lighted as he rode into the main section of town. Hopefully, he looked around for a hotel, a restaurant, unsure if the young frontier town would have either. They were certain to have a saloon or two. Halting briefly in front of the first of these he passed, Tracy called out to a group of men gathered in front of the saloon.

'Where can I stable up my horses?'

'A block ahead, turn down the side street to your right,' one man answered, jabbing a stubby finger in that direction. Another of the group called after him:

'Come back, and bring your wallet.' That tickled the other men enough to start the whole group laughing. Tracy waved a hand and continued on his way.

The stablehand was a woman. She was well into her middle years, had a hundred pounds on Tracy and offered no smile of greeting. She had rough hands, a no-nonsense face, and eyes as sharp as razors. A hard woman doing a hard job in a hard land. Tracy knew better than to try to engage her in conversation. He left his horses with her and strode back uptown toward the sounds of laughter and breaking glass, jeering and whistling, where the night had settled over the saloons, welcoming the would-be revelers.

Tracy found his way inside and settled in near the end of the bar, his hat tilted back on his head. He was wondering how to begin finding answers to his questions. First, however, he let his eyes drift over the crowd. Half of them, at least, seemed to be cattlemen; others farmers, a few shopkeepers. There was no sign of Jack Warren or the bounty hunter's partner, the stubby little man with the quick rifle. Tracy ordered a beer and settled in to watch the men hovering over their card tables or drinking alone, solemnly.

Probably almost all of them knew what had happened to Joe Savage, but that didn't mean they would be responsive if he started asking questions. He was an outsider in the town and most men in these small settlements were mistrustful of strangers. He sure didn't want them to know he was a relative of the famous bandit. Nor could he pose as a lawman. That would probably tighten their jaws quicker than anything.

The decision about which man among the many he might approach for information was soon solved for him. A big-shouldered man in a red and black checked shirt moved to the bar beside Tracy, slapped an empty mug on the counter top, and called out, 'Hey, Gus?

Fill this up, why don't you?'

The stranger had a meaty face with a lopsided smile and gapped front teeth. Glancing sideways at Tracy he looked him up and down and asked, 'Headed for Montana, are you?'

That seemed to be the general impression he made, and Tracy was getting used to it. 'Yes, that's right,' he answered.

'That's all right then. You're welcome here,' the big man said. 'I'm just glad you ain't another one of them bounty hunters.'

'Bounty hunters?' Tracy asked, furrowing his forehead.

'Yeah, they keep popping up. Searching for a man who's already dead.' The big man chuckled, took his filled mug from the bartender and swallowed. 'Crazy idea these men have, thinking that's an easy way to make a living. Riding all the way out here to capture a dead man. No one around here will even tell them where he's buried. Afraid they'll dig up the grave and try to cut off his head or something like that. For identification, you understand?'

'That would be pretty low,' Tracy agreed. 'Also that's a nasty job.'

'They're a pretty nasty bunch from what I've seen of them. You've got to let the dead rest in peace — like the preacher was saying last Sunday.'

'Who are we talking about — the dead man?'

'That's right, you wouldn't know, not being from around here. His name was Joe Savage, and he is most surely dead, and good riddance, although the preacher would also say not to talk ill of the dead.'

'That would be the Reverend Roger Cole?' Tracy asked.

'You know him?' the man asked in surprise.

'In passing,' Tracy said, not embellishing the lie. 'I heard he was over this way.' All he actually knew about the Reverend Mister Cole was that he had a lovely niece named Karin.

'Yeah, he's a good man, but he can

breathe hellfire too. You ought to hear him preach.'

'Maybe I will, but I doubt I'll be around come Sunday.'

'Just a drifting cowboy, huh?'

'That's about it,' Tracy said.

The man scratched his jaw and told Tracy, 'You ought to think about settling down somewhere, you know. The years go by and it makes for tough going sitting that saddle endlessly. You might want to check around here. It's a pretty good little town and a few of the ranchers are trying to replace their own men — everyone's riding to Montana for those high wages, but those boys are losing sight of things that matter. That money won't last them any longer than a cowboy's pay does anywhere.

'You ought to swing by the Rafter T. It's just a little south of here. They'll give you good meals and a soft bunk, and you won't freeze to death come winter. At least look the place over and talk to Amos Tucker. He owns the spread. Like I say, he's going to be short on men.'

'I might do that, thanks.'

Someone called out loudly and gestured impatiently across the room to the big man.

'I got to go now. My seat at the poker table just opened up.'

'I didn't get your name,' Tracy said as the man turned to leave.

'No? I'm sorry. The name is Amos Tucker.' They shook hands briefly, Tucker's big callused hand filling Tracy's grip. He watched the ranch owner go, pondering. Tucker obviously knew quite a bit about local affairs and about Joe Savage. Perhaps in different circumstances he would be willing to talk. And, Tracy considered, he had practically been given an invitation to visit the Rafter T ranch.

Accommodations in Eagle Rock were a little thinner than they were in Baker. Tracy learned that the only place in town to get a meal was where he now stood. The steak served with small boiled potatoes that he ate at a corner table were filling, but the meat was greasy, and the cook apparently had never heard of salt or pepper. Still, it was better than a lot of trail meals Tracy had made for himself.

His meal finished, he asked about getting a place to sleep. Eagle Rock had never had enough people passing through to make a hotel feasible. The townsmen had their own beds in their own small houses; the ranch-hands had their bunks to return to. There was one small 'guest house' which consisted of a single open room with five beds on either side of an aisle. Its customers seemed to be mostly men who were too drunk to make it back to the home ranch.

It would have to do. For a quarter Tracy was given a single gray blanket and his choice of beds. Most army barracks would have put the place to shame, but a man does what he must and Tracy did not forget the many nights he had spent sleeping on the open ground as he rode northward.

He looked around him as he walked toward the last bed on his right, the one nearest the far wall. There was nothing much to be seen. One man had passed out half-in, half-out of his bed. Another sat up, scratching furiously at his head as if he had lice. Another snored so loudly that it was a wonder anyone else could sleep. But Tracy had spent many a night in bunkhouses with the conditions similar if not worse. It did not bother him. One thing did, though:

Where were Jack Warren and his stubby partner on this night? He had half-expected to meet them here, but they were not in the narrow room. Where were they, then, when Tracy had been told there was no other place to hire a bed in Eagle Rock?

Not that he regretted their absence. Who knew what might flare up when they met again?

The lanterns on the wall were turned very low. Tracy hit the bed as the snoring drunk continued his ruckus.

Apparently he now was fighting whiskey demons in his sleep. Tracy could have told him that the demons would win.

Rafter T — now there was something to think about, he thought before going to sleep. Perhaps he could hire on there for a little while. At least until he found out with certainty what had happened to Joe Savage. Tucker knew, he believed. For a dollar a day, meals and a bunk, it would be worth it to ride fence or whatever else Tucker needed done. The wages he had gotten from Double M were not yet gone, but they were critically low.

His choices seemed to be between briefly working at the Rafter T or sitting aimlessly in one of the saloons talking to strangers who seemed disinclined to answer questions about the death of Joe Savage.

A thought came to him unbidden. Had the town itself taken care of Joe Savage? Strung him up as they tired of his criminal activities? It was not unheard of in a small town such as

Eagle Rock where there was no official law. They might have decided to simply eliminate the man, then taken a general vow of silence. Maybe. If so, Tracy only wanted to know. He would figure out what to tell his aunt later. Frontier justice could still be the only justice in many cases, when there was no other sort to appeal to.

He had already decided before he went to sleep. He would ride out to the Rafter T and look the place over, talk to Amos Tucker again. It was that or try to make his way back to Texas with dwindling resources, not even knowing if Justin Mills was hiring at the Double M at this time of year. And that long Texas trail with winter at his back did not sound inviting.

He thought he would write his mother a brief letter in the morning, saying that he had arrived in Wyoming and was still asking around. Maybe that would give the two older women some measure of comfort, just knowing that he was still trying to perform the unfortunate task he had been given.

Tracy was the last one up and out of the 'guest house' in the morning, which surprised him. But then, probably most of the men had work to go to, places they needed to be even if it was only the nearest saloon, whereas he had no particular schedule, no place to go, with the possible exception of the Rafter T, which he still considered the wisest choice. But no one was waiting for him there, and noon was as good as sunrise as far as his plan was concerned.

He still had enough change in his jeans to jingle and so he started up the rutted street again as the morning shadows shortened and the sunlight glittered on the shop windows. There had to be someplace to get breakfast besides the saloon, which, he had decided, badly needed a new cook.

Tracy spotted a young lady in a blue dress standing idly on the corner, hatless, waving a fan in front of her face which was small-featured, round, and tired-appearing. When she looked his way, she smiled brightly, lending Tracy the courage to walk toward her. Where Tracy came from women you did not know were not approached on the street, but this one seemed agreeable enough. Her eyes were drifting up and down the quiet street as Tracy stepped up on to the boardwalk beside her.

'I haven't seen you around before,' she said, still smiling.

'I just drifted up from Texas.'

'Oh, heading for the Montana lands.' She looked him over and added, 'A long time in the saddle, huh?'

'More than I like,' he said. 'Ma'am, I was looking for a place — '

'Lucinda. That's my name, not 'ma'am'.'

'Lucinda, then. I was looking for a place to get some breakfast. I'm new in town, as you know, and the only place I've found that serves food is the saloon.'

'Not very good, is it?' Lucinda said. She continued to scan the street, and continued to wave her fan in front of her face.

'Do you happen to know of a place to eat?'

'Sure. Mona's. I'll take you over there. If you're buying,' Lucinda said, and she took his hand. Her fan was folded now. A slow realization began to steal over Tracy as Lucinda took his hand and started on, leading him.

The fan had been a signal that she was open for business.

Oh, well, it did not matter to Tracy how the woman spent her days or her nights. He only wished to find a decent meal before hitting the trail for the Rafter T ranch. He didn't mind buying her breakfast.

They slipped into a narrow side alley and made their way through the cool, deep shadows. Lucinda had looped her arm around Tracy's, and the gesture did not surprise him, having already deduced what it was Lucinda did to make her way in the world.

Mona's was a tiny place halfway down the alley. It wasn't fancy-looking, but the smells from the kitchen were fresh and enticing. Even at first glance it was obvious that Mona's was a specialized sort of place. With the exception of one old rummy sitting in the corner, head bowed, the rest of the customers were women, some of them dressed only in loose nightdresses. Now and then one of them would rise from a table and walk to a staircase leading to a second story where they presumably had rooms.

It was no real surprise. Tracy knew that any town, whatever its size, would have some similar sort of business venture.

It could also answer the question of where Jack Warren and his pal might have spent last night.

Lucinda had scrambled eggs and crisp bacon which she ate voraciously as if she hadn't had anything to eat for days. Tracy did justice to his four fried eggs and sausage which were prepared very well. Neither spoke during the meal, approaching it as a job to be done. As they sat over coffee, Tracy decided to be audacious and asked:

'Did you know a man called Joe Savage?'

Lucinda choked on her coffee, began coughing and laughing at once and nearly slid off her chair to the floor.

4

'Did I know Joe Savage?' Lucinda asked, using her napkin to wipe the tears of laughter from the corners of her eyes. 'Mister, I could tell you what hat size he took and how he liked his coffee.' Lucinda leaned forward, her eyes intent. 'Please don't tell me I mistook your character. Tell me that you're not one of *them*.'

'Them?'

'Those bounty hunters. The men who wanted to kill him and won't leave him alone now that he's dead. Them that have no more pride than to try to find his grave so they can dig up his bones for money,' Lucinda said heatedly. Her round face was flushed with anger. Tracy decided that the time had come to tell the truth.

'My name is Tracy Keyes. Joe Savage was my cousin,' he told her. He reached into his pocket and retrieved the much-folded telegram from his mother, and gave it to Lucinda to read. She seemed to struggle through it as if she were a woman not used to much reading.

Finally she refolded the yellow paper and slid it back across the table to Tracy.

'I see,' she said in a distant voice. 'Have you come to avenge Joe?'

'No. I don't know who killed him. No one's been willing to tell me. I don't even know for sure that he is dead. Some people seem to doubt it. I was no great friend of Joe Savage. I've come to find an answer for his mother as to what happened to her son. And it's a lot harder going than I imagined it would be.'

'A lot of people are glad it happened,' Lucinda said, 'but I'm not.' Her eyes misted slightly, and she covered her face with her napkin.

'You liked Joe?'

'Yes, I liked him!' she said, her voice rising. 'He was a good, generous man.'

Tracy thought the emphasis had been on 'generous', but he said nothing. Around them other women rose and started for the stairway. A few of them smiled warmly at Tracy, which gave his spirits a temporary boost until he remembered that the women were working, and smiles were a part of their craft.

'You can't guess who killed Joe?' Tracy asked. 'Or why?'

'I can't guess who it was,' Lucinda replied, 'but I'll bet they wanted to rob him. Everyone said he had a lot of money he'd collected in some of his 'adventures'. That's what Joe always called them — adventures.'

'So you think he had a lot of money stashed away?'

'I *know* he did,' Lucinda said, 'but he had spent it all, or most of it, by the time he was killed.'

'Was he a gambler?'

Lucinda smiled distantly. 'No more so than anyone else, but that's not what he did with his money. He bought a little piece of land, forty acres. We had decided to get out of our . . . businesses and go straight, build a little house on the land.'

'Oh?' Tracy frowned. And who owned the land now — Lucinda? Or would it fall to Joe Savage's heirs — his mother, Enora Savage, or other heirs . . . even to his cousin? Tracy wondered if there was a will. Not that he wanted the property, nor would Enora, but if it could be sold for a small profit, she, a widow, could probably use the money.

He probed a little further. 'Where was this property?' he asked. Lucinda's eyes were far away in some place where dreams actually did come true.

'What?' she asked as if she had been awakened. 'Oh, the property. In the loveliest place imaginable. Up near Mirror Lake. Set on a hillside overlooking it through the pines.'

It was *where?* On the site where Karin Cole had told him her uncle meant to build a chapel? She had told him there were problems associated. A problem about legal ownership, with Joe Savage dead and unable to dispute any claim? Perhaps he should talk to Karin again. He had no idea where she lived, but everyone seemed to know where and when Reverend Cole held his meetings. Karin surely would attend her uncle's services.

It seemed that Joe Savage was causing as much trouble dead as he had when he was alive.

Lucinda looked at the pretty little gold watch she had pinned to her bodice and rose with an apology.

'I thank you for breakfast, but I really have to be getting to work, unless you . . . ?'

Tracy shook his head. Perhaps in another time, another place, but he, too, had work to attend to. He got to his feet as Lucinda rose, placing her napkin on the table.

At almost the same moment, Tracy heard the heavy clumping of boot leather on the steps and he turned his head to see Jack Warren, adjusting his collar, his coat over his arm, and his stubby, bald friend coming down toward the room. An unseen woman called out from above in farewell.

Jack Warren came down three more steps before his eyes, habitually, it seemed, swept the restaurant and he spotted Tracy Keyes.

'I should've known you'd be here,' Warren growled. 'Didn't I tell you to stay off my backtrail?'

There was no sense in arguing with the man or in explaining. 'I'm leaving,' he said, nudging Lucinda aside, not knowing what Warren might have in mind.

'That's not good enough,' the man with the long black mustache said, coming down the last few steps, his friend, his face now flushed crimson with anger, at his heels. His hand was dangling near his holstered pistol. 'I want you out of this town in five minutes or less,' Warren said.

Lucinda had paused near the foot of the stairs. Now she hoisted her skirts and hustled up them toward the rooms overhead.

Jack Warren's hand now settled onto the butt of his Colt and a shriek, a lioness's roar sounded from near the kitchen door. 'Oh, no!' the woman bellowed threateningly. 'Not in my place, you don't!'

Tracy glanced at the woman — Mona? — who had appeared among them. She was grossly fat, her eyes almost lost in the folds of the flesh around them. Her body was round — not full, but almost exactly round. A ball with tiny legs and heavy, flaccid arms jutting from it.

'If there's any shooting in my place, they'll close me down, you moron. Especially since the whole town has suddenly caught religion. I won't have it, you hear? I won't! Take it outside, whatever it is!' She stamped her foot to emphasize her point. Two burly men in white aprons had emerged from the kitchen to stand scowling beside her.

'Ah, forget it,' Jack Warren said with a little laugh.

His partner wasn't that willing to let it go. The stubby, bald-headed man squeaked out a taunt and charged across the restaurant floor toward Tracy, scattering the remaining girls, who retreated with shrieks and a rustle of garments. Jack Warren did not join in; neither did he try to do anything to halt his friend's headlong rush toward Tracy Keyes.

The little man bowled into Tracy, turning over a chair and a table in his mindless charge. Tracy was driven back against the wall. Mona — if that was she — growled out another scream. The women who were left in the room withdrew to the corners or into the kitchen. Tracy found himself upright, pressed between the wall and the bald man, who stuck two hard hooks into his ribs, one on either side of his body.

Tracy had his arms free and before the stubby man could do further damage, brought his forearm down across the bridge of his attacker's nose. Bone broke, and blood gushed from the man's nostrils, but it did nothing to slow his assault. His fury was not understandable. You would have thought Tracy had done him some unforgivable wrong.

The bald man continued to thump his fists into Tracy's mid-section. Anyone who deduced that the man had no strength, using his stature as criteria, would have been wrong. There was plenty of hard muscle in the bald-headed man's shoulders and he was enjoying using Tracy as a punching bag, no matter that his own face was smeared with blood.

One left-handed shot caught Tracy joltingly in the liver, and he decided that he had had enough. He turned and twisted to back away from his attacker and give himself room to work. Tracy was no skilled fighter, but the years on the range and in bunkhouse scuffles had given him a knowledge of the basics.

He stamped the heel of his boot down roughly on the bald man's foot, and when the man bent over in pain, Tracy wound up and threw an uppercut through his defenses, catching him on the point of his chin, clattering his teeth together. When the stubby man straightened up this time, his hands hung loosely at his sides. Tracy took aim and threw two head-snapping straight left-handed shots into the man's already pulverized face. Then he stepped back for a finishing right hook.

It was not needed. The bald man's eyes were rolled back in his skull, and with a little animal-like whimper, he went to his knees and then to the floor of the restaurant. Mona rushed toward them as soon as the fight had ended.

'Take him out of here! I have a business here. Take him out and don't come back!' she screamed. Tracy recovered his hat, wiped back his hair and planted his Stetson.

'He's not my dog,' Tracy said. He jabbed a finger at Jack Warren. 'Let *him* take him home.'

Then he turned and pushed his way

through the door as Mona watched, hands on hips.

The front of Tracy's shirt was smeared with his adversary's blood. He hated to waste any of the little money he had left, but he decided that he should purchase yet another new one, especially if he were going out to the Rafter T to speak with Amos Tucker, which was his plan for the morning.

No one so much as glanced at him as he strode up the main street toward the dry-goods store. There was a white moon riding high in the pale sky like a disinterested observer. Tracy bought a shirt with small checks of blue and white, and pearl snaps on the front and the cuffs. He was debating whether or not to throw his old shirt away when the man working in the store offered:

'I can have that cleaned inside of four hours.'

Tracy agreed, left the shirt there and walked out into the glare of the morning sun once more.

The girl popped up in the oddest places.

Karin Cole stood on the boardwalk, the shade of the awning darkening her copper-colored hair. In her hands was a sheaf of papers. Tracy walked up to her. Startled, she took her eyes off the street traffic and turned toward him, holding the papers to her breast.

'It's you,' she said breathlessly. 'I didn't expect to see you again.'

'Well, here I am — I haven't made it to Montana yet.'

'Is that where you're going?' Karin asked.

'Not really, but it's what everyone assumes. What are you doing in town?'

'Handing these out,' she said, showing him one of the papers she was still clasping to her body. They were notices for a church meeting to be held at the home of Mr and Mrs George Parker — whoever they were.

'Having any luck?' he asked mildly.

'I have a dozen or so people interested. At least they said they were.

Some of these cowboys . . . '

'You think they just wanted an excuse to talk to you?' Tracy suggested.

'Well, yes!' she admitted with a short laugh.

'You can't blame them much,' Tracy said, studying Karin a little more closely until she began to blush. 'Where's your uncle? Shouldn't he be helping you with this?'

'He's home working on this Sunday's sermon. He's hoping to shake the local citizens free of some of their money so that we can start building the chapel. That didn't sound right, did it?' she asked.

'No, but that's how churches get built, isn't it? Has he thrown a lot of hellfire into his sermon this week?'

'Has he . . . ? That's a terrible way to put it,' Karin said, frowning.

'Sorry. I had someone tell me that that was one of the reverend's specialties.'

'Well, it's not,' Karin said. 'His sermons are deeply moving and

. . . spiritual.' She was protective of her uncle's reputation, it seemed. Well, that was how it should be. 'Do you think we'll be seeing you? On Sunday?'

'I don't know,' Tracy said, taking the announcement she had pressed on him. 'I don't mind religion — but churches seem to make me kind of nervous.'

'I can't understand that.'

'Neither can I, really, but they do,' Tracy said. 'Besides, I may be working on Sunday.'

'You've found a situation?' she asked, and her blue eyes were bright, seemingly hopeful.

'It's not certain yet, but I may be riding for Amos Tucker's Rafter T.'

'Then you can bring him along to the Parker house. He knows where it is,' Karin said eagerly.

'We'll have to see about that,' Tracy answered, folding the bulletin away to place in his shirt pocket. 'Like I say, I may be working.'

'A man should keep holy the Sabbath

day. You should not be working on Sundays,' she said a little archly, as if some of her uncle's training had rubbed off on her.

'The cows don't know that,' Tracy said with a grin.

She offered her hand briefly as they said goodbye. Tracy took a dozen strides down along the boardwalk and stopped to glance back. Karin was watching him, but she turned her eyes away quickly when he caught her at it.

What the hell, he thought. What was one Sunday out of his life?

If Amos Tucker made him an offer of employment he could simply tell him that he couldn't start until Monday. If Tucker asked him why, going to church was an honorable enough excuse. But Tracy was getting ahead of himself. Tucker's offer had been made off-handedly, and possibly had been saloon-influenced. Besides, his own idea of going to see Tucker again had been based on the thought that Tucker knew what had happened to the mysterious Joe Savage. He believed that Tucker knew more. Whether he would talk about it was moot.

The most likely answer to the death of Joe Savage, was one already presented to Tracy. The town, tiring of Savage's crooked ways, had banded together and decided to string him up from some lonesome tree. No one in Eagle Rock would be willing to admit complicity in such an act.

But there had to be an answer, and Tracy was bound by blood and his given word to discover what it was, no matter how long it took or who it incriminated.

For one thing was certain — whatever had become of Joe Savage, it had been murder. His personality would never allow thoughts of suicide. No, the Joe Savage that Tracy knew would do anything to cling to life. A violent struggle would have been needed to take the outlaw down.

There was a murderer loose in this remote mountain town.

5

The ride to the Rafter T was hot and dusty. The ranch house was only five miles from Eagle Rock, but on this day, with his ribs bruised and his back and liver complaining, it was almost all that Tracy could do to sit the saddle for that long a ride.

He still did not understand why the stubby little man had attacked him so violently. Was it because they suspected that Tracy was trying to poach on Joe Savage's bounty, which they had claimed for their own? That seemed the most likely explanation.

Tracy began to see scattered cattle grazing their patient, bovine way across the dry-grass flats ahead of him. He passed through a large grouping of dusty live-oak trees and found himself looking at the house of Amos Tucker. It was not what he had expected.

The house was built in the style of a Mexican ranchero with open balconies, arched doorways and pillared supports. It was much smaller than the grand mansions of those he had seen on the land-grant ranches in Mexico when he had pushed Double M cattle across the border with Justin Mills, but it was large for this part of the country. Tracy wondered idly where Tucker had gotten the adobe to build his house, that type of clay not being native to Wyoming. It did seem that Amos Tucker was comfortably well-to-do; however, if he now could not keep his hired hands around, Tracy could see that there might soon be a sort of crisis in handling the herd.

Yet 'Gone to Montana' seemed to be the byword of the times. Tucker had been right about that, Tracy knew: no matter how inflated the pay was on those northern ranches, the money would last the cowhands no longer than it did anywhere else and their hardships would be doubled.

To the side of the L-shaped house there was a fountain surrounded by Spanish tile. In one of the sheltered doorways, Amos Tucker stood watching Tracy's approach.

The rancher wore a black suit, white shirt, and was without a tie. His broad face reflected curiosity and then broke into a grin. He gestured toward an unseen person and came forward to meet Tracy in the sunlight. The fountain burbled and filled the air with cooling mist as it trickled down the tiers of clamshell-shaped ornamentation. Tucker watched Tracy swing down stiffly from Thunder's back.

'Well — I'm glad you decided to stop by,' Tucker said in a booming greeting. He offered Tracy his hand. 'You got yourself a little beat up since the last time I saw you.'

'I'm sore, that's all,' Tracy said.

'Let's go inside where it's cooler and talk,' Tucker suggested. 'Will your horse stand? He can drink out of the fountain. That's about all it's good for anyway!'

Tracy told Turner that the sorrel would stay where it was left, and before they had entered the house, Thunder was helping himself to the cool water that flowed from the fountain.

The furniture scattered around the cavernous rooms inside the house was also of Spanish style: heavy, dark wood, which matched the house's character. The room they entered had a huge arched fireplace set into a white-plastered wall. A few Indian blankets decorated the walls. Tucker waved a hand toward a couch and sat down in a heavy dark chair with a high, carved back. His eyes still studied Tracy's movements which were stiff and cautious.

'Who was it?' Tucker asked, leaning forward, his big hands dangling.

'Who was what?'

'Who was it that beat you? Son, I've lived in hard lands for a long time. I know the signs. Who was it?'

'You wouldn't know them,' Tray said.

'Try me.'

'All right,' Tracy Keyes said with a

sigh which made his sore ribs twinge just a little. 'It was a man named Jack Warren and a little bald man whose name I don't know. They are bounty hunters. They jumped me in a place called Mona's — or rather the bald man did while Warren watched.'

'Mona's?' Tucker asked. He obviously knew of the establishment.

'I just went in for breakfast. I couldn't find another place,' Tracy said defensively.

'It's all right with me,' Tucker said, holding up a hand. 'I don't pass judgement on men. We all need . . . The bald man's name is Reginald Goode, more commonly called 'Porky'.'

'Porky? He has a little problem with his temper. Tell me, Mr Tucker, would those two really go so far as to dig up Joe Savage's body so that it could be identified for the bounty?'

'I don't know them *that* well,' Tucker answered. 'Let's just say it wouldn't be beyond them.'

'Who knows where Joe Savage is

buried?' Tracy asked.

'Boy, you're starting to sound like a bounty hunter yourself — or a lawman,' Tucker said a little roughly.

'I'm neither, believe me.' Since he had already shown the telegram to Lucinda, and because he sincerely liked Amos Tucker and desired his good opinion, Tracy once again drew the telegram from his mother out of his pocket and passed it over to the silent ranch owner.

'Joe Savage is your cousin?' Tucker said in a startled manner.

'Yes. He was not like a brotherly sort of cousin. I haven't seen him in years, you understand, and even then we didn't get along. It's a matter of family loyalty that has brought me all the way up here.'

'I see,' Tucker said, slumping down in his chair, the telegram dangling between his fingers. 'Yes, things make perfect sense now. His mother wants to know if he's alive or dead, and where he's buried if he is not alive.'

'That's it — if it were up to me, I'd shrug and ride away. I never did like Joe Savage much, even as a boy.'

'I think that Joe Savage didn't like himself much as he grew older, what he had become — at least that was the Reverend Cole's belief.'

'The two men met each other?' Tracy asked with disbelief. Why would Joe Savage ever approach a man of the cloth? Of course it could be as Tucker had said, maybe Joe had seen the end of the trail he was traveling and was trying to reform.

'Apparently they were quite close. Joe gave up his claim to the land up near Mirror Lake for the minister to build his chapel on.'

Thinking about it, that was about the only use for that parcel. It was pretty enough, in its way, but the timber there could be cleared out in a week. It would never be farmland or large enough for cattle or horses to be run. But Lucinda had said that Joe was intent on building a house for the two of them up there.

That may have been just the hopeful belief of a woman who had little else to hope for. Or Joe could have been flat-out lying to her.

'Is that where he's buried?' Tracy asked quietly.

Tucker glanced around as if someone might be eavesdropping. 'Yes,' he said. 'The reverend calls the place Missionary Ridge now, but it's Joe's old spread.'

Joe Savage, who was apparently ready to put away his guns and settle down, giving his land away, to a church? It was hard to believe. Tucker must have seen the disbelief on Tracy's face.

'That's what happened, according to the Reverend Cole.' He handed the telegram back to Tracy. 'Perhaps his mother would like to know that. You know, Tracy, religion and guilt can affect some men pretty strongly. As strongly as liquor. They need to make amends and don't know how.'

'It's still hard to believe that Joe . . . ' Especially if he was sincere about settling down with Lucinda. But who knew if he had been? Tracy had never known Joe well enough to hazard a guess about his motives.

'Well,' Tucker said as if it made him uncomfortable, 'there was also the understanding that the reverend's niece was to marry Joe. What is her name?'

'Karin,' Tracy provided.

'That's right, she was a part of the bargain.'

That made more sense to Tracy. He couldn't see Joe Savage having an attack of remorse and guilt and handing his property over to the church. If it was barter for Cole's niece, however, he could understand. The little copper-haired girl was worth more than forty acres on a hilltop. The idea depressed Tracy. What sort of man was Roger Cole if he had agreed to such a plan — exchanging his niece for a chapel?

But perhaps the two events had simply occurred simultaneously, without a grand scheme. The reverend looking for a building site; Karin falling for Joe Savage. *I was not there*, Tracy Keyes had to remind himself forcefully. He could not judge people's motives from this distance.

'I'm sorry,' Amos Tucker said, 'I'm sure you were looking for more answers, but that is all I know of the entire business.'

Tracy nodded, rose and tucked the telegram away in his shirt pocket once again. He started toward the door to the big house, then paused and asked, 'Was it the town that did it, Mr Tucker? Was it the town of Eagle Rock that took Joe Savage out and executed him?'

Tucker shook his head heavily. 'I don't know, Tracy. I've heard rumors to that effect, but I have no personal knowledge of anything like that happening. And,' he added, 'I think it's a waste of your time to try to find anyone who would admit to it, if it's true.'

'I know,' Tracy said as they stepped out into the bright, cool day. Thunder still stood untied near the fountain. The horse glanced in their direction curiously.

'Well, we've gotten everything settled except for the main reason I summoned you,' Amos Tucker said, throwing a friendly arm across Tracy's shoulders. 'I've been losing men right and left as they go off to Montana seeking that big payday. Have you decided whether or not you would like to work for me?'

'No, sir — not exactly. As you know I've got other matters to attend to.'

'So you're still not satisfied?'

'No, sir, you've been helpful, but it is not over. There is a secret behind the death of Joe Savage, and I won't be satisfied until I unearth it.'

Tucker nodded and answered, 'Just be careful, Tracy. You are still following an unknown trail.' As Tracy swung aboard Thunder, the ranch owner asked, 'Can I do anything else to help you out?'

'Maybe so. One thing, Mr Tucker. I've another horse. A mare. Her name's Changa. She's a calm little white animal. But if I keep her stabled up much longer, the livery fees are going to drain my pockets of the little cash I have left.

'As I said, she's a mare, but I don't think it's her time of the year yet, and if she could be kept away from any stallions you may have around, she wouldn't be a bit of trouble.'

'Of course, of course!' Tucker said jovially. 'I'll take her feed out of your first month's pay.'

Tucker seemed to be assuming that Tracy would stay in Wyoming rather than take a long dry ride to Texas, his pockets empty, without the certainty of finding a job when he reached the Double M. That could be the way it would work out, Tracy thought, but he wanted the choice to be his option.

'Don't worry about the mare,' Tucker said as Tracy turned the sorrel to leave. 'I've got a yard boy who would be happy to go to town and pick her up.'

Then the man stood, hands on hips, watching as Tracy rode away, feeling better, but no wiser after his conversation with the Rafter T owner. Looking back Tracy saw Tucker still standing beneath the portico, hands on his hips. His expression was unreadable, but odd for a man who had just said a pleasant farewell. Had anything Tucker told him been the truth? Had he made a mistake in showing the rancher the telegram?

There was no way of being certain. One thing was for sure — someone in this little town, perhaps everyone, was holding something back from Tracy Keyes.

★ ★ ★

He met them on his way into Eagle Rock, riding in a little surrey with a fancy, impossibly glossy black horse pulling it along the dusty road. Tracy drew Thunder to the side. It was the two people in Eagle Rock that he most wanted to talk to, but at the pace the horse was moving, they had no time for conversation on this day. Perhaps they never would.

Karin Cole sat erectly on the carriage bench, her hands folded between her knees. She wore a bright yellow dress and a straw hat with a matching yellow band. The man driving the surrey was somber in manner, dark-eyed, and critical-looking. This, Tracy knew, had to be the Reverend Mister Cole. His beard was long and straight, reminding Tracy of engravings he had seen of the abolitionist, John Brown. His eyes were sheltered behind a pair of rimless spectacles. Tracy could see the hellfire in the man; it seemed to almost encircle him as an aura of menace. Tracy, without reason, had been expecting a twinkling-eyed, white-haired, pudgy little man.

He could see Karin nudging her uncle with her elbow, saying something rapidly to him and with a sort of bitter shrug, Reverend Cole slowed the surrey and eventually brought it to a halt beside Tracy.

Karin, her voice more restrained on this morning, made the introductions. 'Tracy, this is my uncle, Roger Cole. Uncle, this is the man I told you about, Tracy Keyes.'

'Keyes?' the preacher said in a gravelly voice. 'I don't know anyone named Keyes.'

'Of course not,' Karin said lightly. 'I told you he's just arrived. He's on his way to Montana.'

'Yes, yes, I remember now,' Cole said irritably. 'What is it you wanted to talk to us about?'

Bluntly, Tracy said, 'Joe Savage.'

He thought he saw the eyes behind the preacher's spectacles react, but it might have just been that he found the subject unpleasant. It could also be that he knew quite a bit about Joe Savage, including how the land on what was now known as Missionary Ridge had been transferred to him — if indeed it had been. One more matter Tracy meant to look into. Perhaps with Joe

Savage gone the preacher had simply laid claim to the property. He had no reason to doubt the man, and he hated casting aspersions on a man of religion, but then history was speckled with examples of misdeeds by certain 'holy men'.

Now Roger Cole sighed deeply, brushed the back of his hand across his long, straight beard and told Tracy, 'I knew Joe Savage. He first came around because of Karin, I suspect. But over the days, weeks, months I knew him we began talking seriously. I managed to convince him of the grievous errors in the way he had conducted his life.

'There was no single moment I can point to, but in the end Joe renounced his life of crime and repented of his sinfulness.'

'Joe Savage?' Tracy asked in disbelief. Karin frowned at him; the Reverend Cole's eyes bored holes in him.

'Do you have no belief in salvation?' Cole asked. 'Is a sinner always to be condemned by certain mistakes he has made in his life? Is there no such thing as heartfelt repentance? If not,' Cole added dolefully, 'all in my profession, of any faith, are doomed to failure and any religion becomes an exercise in futility.'

This was deep going for Tracy and he decided not to debate with the preacher. 'And he just turned over the forty acres up along Missionary Ridge to you?'

'Joe wanted others to have a place to go and discover the peace he had found in repentance. The chapel was to be a gesture of atonement for his past.'

Tracy had no reason to doubt the man, but he did. He looked at Karin, who, astonishingly, blushed. Yes, she had been a part of the bargain, of that Tracy was suddenly sure. There was little more to ask, and Cole was clearly tired of the conversation anyway.

'Now, if you will excuse us, we have to prepare for a church function at George Parker's home. They have generously offered to allow us to use it for our services until the funds for the chapel can be found and the building completed.'

With that Cole gathered up the reins again. Tracy asked a last question in parting:

'Is Joe Savage really dead?'

'Is he . . . ' The preacher's face was flaming. 'We buried him on Missionary Ridge as he requested. I spoke over his grave myself.'

'Who killed him? Sir?' Cole had started his horse along the road. Tracy called out once again. 'Sir! Who killed Joe Savage?' But he was speaking only to a stream of dust rising from the wheels of the surrey. 'I don't seem to have handled that real well,' Tracy muttered to Thunder. The horse was indifferent to the comment. Tracy started it on along the short distance back to Eagle Rock.

It was still only the middle of the afternoon. Perhaps, he thought, he could manage to find the town recorder's office and see who actually held the title to that piece of land up above Mirror Lake. It was possible that Joe Savage had died before he had the chance to transfer the title to Reverend Cole — that could explain the delay in getting the chapel built.

It was also possible that Joe never intended to do so at all. That his 'gesture of atonement' had been a sham to ingratiate himself with Karin's uncle. That would fit together with Lucinda's version of what Joe had planned for that land. Did she even know about Karin Cole? He supposed so. A woman who knew your hat size would probably know that much.

Tracy needed to talk to Lucinda once more, but he did not want to infuriate Mona by showing up at her establishment again. He imagined Lucinda could be found around the local saloons at night, or that someone who knew her could be. He would go looking for her after he finished searching the records in the town's land office.

This job, difficult from the inception,

had snarled upon itself crazily. If he had any sense, Tracy reflected, he would just ride out and send a letter to his mother, telling her that he had tried and failed to find out a thing about Joe Savage. He couldn't swallow the lie, however; he had learned more about Joe Savage in two days than he could have imagined. Unfortunately, Joe had led such a tangled life that he still could not even tell his mother and Aunt Enora whether he was alive or dead, or where he was buried.

The easiest way out would be to take the Reverend Cole at his word and send his letter to fit that explanation, but it was difficult to make Cole's story fit in with certain other facts Tracy knew.

Well — he yawned widely, still sitting his saddle in front of the recorder's office — one thing at a time. Swinging down, he went through the sun-blistered green door and into the dark interior.

6

'No!' the county recorder said with vehemence. 'Unless you're a lawyer or you have a badge to show me, I can't let you go pawing through town documents.' He was not a little, shy man as Tracy had expected. The city clerk behind the desk was taller than Tracy, and broader. His face was set in a scowl. The country around seemed to be shy of small men. Tracy tried again.

'I thought these things were a matter of public record,' Tracy said. 'Other places I've been — '

'This ain't any other place. It's Eagle Rock, and that's the way we do business here.'

Tracy tipped back his hat, placed his forearms on the counter and tried an appeasing smile. 'Look, mister, all I want to know is who owns a certain piece of property. Or did own it, since it seems he's dead. I represent his family, and they're interested in matters. If the man hasn't sold it, the ownership might fall to them.'

'I see,' the clerk said. His glare had softened slightly. 'Who's the man we're talking about?'

'Joe Savage,' Tracy told him and the sour expression returned to the clerk's face.

'You're kin to Joe Savage?'

'I am,' Tracy had to admit. 'His cousin.'

'And what kind of trick are you trying to pull on me? Shouldn't you be out there robbing and shooting some-one?'

'I'm not trying any tricks,' Tracy said, letting the other part of the man's angry little speech pass. 'The land might belong to Joe's mother, my aunt, if he never got around to transferring the title to someone else. She's a widow and could use the money it would bring at sale. Couldn't you at least look it up and tell me that much?'

'You know how much I would do for Joe Savage or anyone related to that skunk?' the clerk asked. Then he turned his head and spat quite deliberately on the floor.

This was not going to work. There had to be someone in town who would listen to him. Didn't they at least have a mayor, a judge? 'Who runs this town?' Tracy asked, his own smile faded.

'As far as you're concerned, I do. Now, if you don't mind stepping out? You're holding up business.'

There was no one else in the small office, but there was nothing to be gained by bandying words with the stubborn clerk. Well, he had tried. Tracy went out into the sunlight again. Already the shadows stretching out from the bases of the building were growing long, pooling in the alleys. He began walking his horse toward the stable. As he went, he pondered what his next move should be. It seemed he was running in circles. What had he really learned? Every time he thought he had some solid information, the next person he met contradicted it.

He had to talk to Lucinda again, he decided. Inside the stable he whistled up the worker. As he waited for the stablehand to appear, he looked around, noticing that Changa was gone. He asked the hand, a man he had not seen before, about the white mare.

'Yeah, a kid came in from the Rafter T and took it with him.' A shadow of doubt crossed his narrow face. 'That was all right, wasn't it? He said Amos Tucker sent him.'

'It was all right,' Tracy assured him. 'Now if you'll see to my sorrel, I'll be all set.'

'Is it going to spend the night?' the man asked Tracy.

Was it? Was *he*? He supposed so. It was a long ride back to the Rafter T on a weary horse. And he still wanted to talk to Lucinda again. 'Yes, we'll be staying over,' Tracy said. Even if it meant spending anther night in the shabby, noisy 'guest house' down the street.

Walking back along the street he looked into two saloons, but did not see Lucinda. The sun was low behind the buildings and the sky was beginning to color. It was nearly suppertime. He decided to make his way back to Mona's. Lucinda was likely taking her evening meal about now. Mona had warned him to stay away from her place, but what could she do except order him out again?

There had to be another door, didn't there? At least for deliveries to the kitchen and taking the trash out. He passed the front door to Mona's as a man came out, picking his teeth. Tracy did not know him. They only glanced at each other and kept going on their way. The smell of roast beef was in the air, and Tracy's stomach reacted with a rumbling.

Coming to a cross-alley, Tracy saw what he had expected. There was a door to this alley as well, fully closed

101

now, and a set of wooden stairs leading up to the second floor where the girls had their rooms.

Someone was sitting on the second lowest step. Tracy walked that way, seeing that it was a young woman, no more than twenty years of age. She wore blue jeans and a white shirt. She was slender, had large dark eyes, and wore her hair drawn back on her small skull and arranged in some sort of feminine fashion. She did not rise as Tracy approached her through the shadows, but her expression was one of someone who would rather not be there at this particular moment.

Tracy walked toward her and halted about six feet away. He tried a smile.

'Are you staying here?' he asked.

'I work here,' she answered in a musical but wary voice.

'Do you?' Tracy asked, studying her. She didn't seem the type.

'I clean the rooms — make the beds, clear out the whiskey bottles and empty the ashtrays. Just an ordinary maid.

Mona is my aunt.'

'Really?' Tracy could see no resemblance to the fat woman who ran the place. 'I'd never have guessed that.'

'You might have if you'd seen Mona about a hundred pounds ago.'

Or more, Tracy thought but did not say. 'My name is Tracy Keyes. What's yours, if you don't mind telling me?'

'Melanie Douglas.'

'Miss Douglas, I was looking for someone. Maybe you can help me.'

'Who?' Melanie asked mistrustfully.

'A girl named Lucinda.' A little hiss of breath passed through Melanie's teeth.

'What is it?' Tracy asked. 'Don't you like Lucinda?'

'I don't like any of the girls here,' Melanie told him coldly. 'They all think they're getting ahead in the world when all they're doing is throwing their lives away.'

'I see — I really would like to find Lucinda, though. I still have some unfinished business I want to discuss with her.'

'I understand,' Melanie said, looking past Tracy now at the reddish glow in the sky.

'I don't think you do,' Tracy said. 'This is strictly business.'

'Everything Lucinda does is strictly business,' Melanie said, now rising, her gaze returning to Tracy's face.

'No, this is quite different,' Tracy explained. 'A relative of mine is missing, and Lucinda told me that she knew him. I still haven't been able to find him, so I decided to talk to her again. Maybe she forgot something important, something that would help me out.'

'Is this where she met him?' Melanie asked, tossing her head toward the building beside her.

'I don't really know. I suppose so.'

Melanie paused, arranging her thoughts. It was obvious that she didn't like giving out information about Mona's place. She nodded shortly. She must have decided that Tracy was on the level, for she told him:

'She just finished eating and left. She usually goes to the Bluebird at this time of the evening.' Tracy's face must have been blank, for she added, 'The Bluebird Saloon. There's a sign on the place. It's right up the street. If you can't find it just ask any of our local loafers and boozers.'

'You don't like this town much, do you?'

'What is there to like?' she asked in return. 'Good luck to you, Mr Keyes. I have to get back to work now.'

Tracy watched her ascend the stairs, her little boots making clicking sounds on the planks. She paused just for a moment on the landing, looked down at Tracy, then went quickly into the building, closing the door deliberately behind her. Tracy's eyebrows arched in a slight frown, then he shrugged and walked away again, heading back toward the main street of Eagle Rock.

With the end of the day, the saloons were coming to life. Loud shouts and curses and bursts of wild laughter met

Tracy's ears as he walked the board-walk, looking for the sign that advertised the Bluebird Saloon. When he did find it, he noticed that there were two bullet holes in the wooden sign. The men of Eagle Rock took their fun seriously, it seemed.

Shouldering his way through the saloon door, Tracy saw Lucinda almost immediately. She was wearing a dark green silky dress. Her head was thrown back in laughter. Two men were standing with her, and as Tracy approached it was obvious they did not want to share her company.

'Please,' Tracy said to Lucinda. 'Can we talk?'

'Find your own girl to talk to,' one of the men with her growled. A big man with an unkempt mustache which drooped over his mouth.

Lucinda put her hand on the big man's forearm, restraining him. 'Please, Lou, this is business.'

'I thought we were discussing business,' Lou responded.

'This is completely different. Please! I'll come right back as soon as I'm through talking to this man.' Lou grumbled an answer and withdrew, looking back over his shoulder as he left.

'He's pretty possessive for a poor man,' Lucinda said. She smiled as if something about what she had said amused her. Tracy noticed that her glass was empty and asked:

'Can I buy you another drink?'

'I guess you can. Pick out a table and I'll come on over shortly.'

'How much for a drink?' Tracy asked, sorting out his change.

'Fifty cents will do it,' Lucinda said. He gave her two quarters and watched as she swayed away toward the bar. One of the quarters, he noticed, was pocketed along the way. Well, a girl has to make a living.

He found a small square table in the far corner of the room. There was a window there, but it had been painted over a long time ago. Men's initials were scratched in the green paint, as they were in the top of the cigarette-scarred table. Lucinda was back almost as soon as Tracy had taken a seat in the wooden chair. He didn't bother to rise to pull her chair out for her. He doubted that this bit of etiquette was practiced much in here.

Lucinda put her drink on the table, swept her skirt into position and sat down facing him, her eyes sparkling with excitement or with liquor. She wore a smile still. 'What is this about? It has to be about Joe Savage — that's it, isn't it? Have you found out something?'

'A lot of nothing,' Tracy replied. 'Except for the Reverend Cole who swears that he buried Joe himself, up on Missionary Ridge.'

'Don't call our property that,' Lucinda said sharply.

'Sorry. I just try to go along with local usage. Tell me, Lucinda,' Tracy said, lifting his eyes to look around the rowdy barroom, 'when was the last time you actually saw Joe Savage in the flesh?'

Lucinda seemed to think that was amusing too. But after a few moments she answered seriously. 'It's been over a year now. At the beginning of last summer. We were in . . . my room just talking and Joe told me he was sorry but he had to leave for a little while. He said that he had one more adventure lined up — I told you that was how he described his work, didn't I — as adventures?'

Tracy nodded and let Lucinda go on. Her eyes were distinctly unhappy now as she was forced to retreat in time to a painful conversation.

'I asked him not to go, but he told me it was already set up. I knew I couldn't talk him out of anything once he had his mind made up to do it.' Lucinda finished her drink in one swallow. She told Tracy seriously, 'Joe told me — he promised me — that when he came back he would have enough money for us to live on for years. Then he was going to build the little house we had agreed up by Mirror Lake. We could both get out of our businesses and live like regular human beings.'

'He was sincere, was he?'

'Oh, quite sincere,' Lucinda said, meeting Tracy's gaze directly.

Then why had the land been transferred to Reverend Cole? If it had been. Tracy had seen no legal document of any kind. Had Cole just stolen the land? That was a dark view to take of the preacher, but all things were possible. Where, he wondered, had Joe Savage gone on this adventure? Perhaps he had tried to stick up a bank or rob a train and been killed far from Eagle Rock. But Reverend Cole was positive that Joe was buried up by Mirror Lake. Lucinda had been watching his eyes as if she could see his thoughts.

'Can't make no sense out of it, huh?' she said quietly.

'No, I can't.'

'If Joe was alive, Tracy, I tell you this — he would have come to see me.' This was said with a sort of false confidence. 'One thing Joe told me that has helped. I asked him did he want me to move out of Mona's and find some other kind of work. Joe told me there was time for reforming later. He said he didn't want me to just quit working and then sit alone, looking out the window, waiting for him.'

'So you just kept on . . . ?'

'Just kept on working. These men you see around here, they're not handsome, not smart, but just being around them puts a little life in my world.'

Tracy saw that her eyes were tearing up just a little, and her lower lip was beginning to tremble. Had it occurred to her as it had to Tracy that that might have been Joe's way of giving her the brush-off?

Since he couldn't think of anything else to ask her just then, he rose to leave. Across the room, the man named Lou was glaring at him, his eyes going from Tracy to Lucinda who now did seem to be on the verge of tears.

'I'll be going now, Lucinda. Maybe I can see you again — if I find out anything.'

'I'll be mad if you don't tell me whatever you find out,' she said, her voice rising a little. Tracy left her sitting alone at the table and made his way toward the front door.

He should have expected it, but he didn't. As he stepped out into the evening, Lou was there, waiting for him, his shoulders hunched, his fists bunched tightly. Tracy turned away and started in the opposite direction, but Lou shouted after him.

'Just hold it right there!' A few men had gathered around curiously, most with beer mugs in their hands. Lou stalked to where Tracy stood waiting.

'Can I help you?' Tracy asked calmly.

'I saw you making Lucinda cry,' the big man said in a voice that was like a grizzly bear huffing. 'Everyone around here likes Lucinda — whatever you were saying to her, you shouldn't have done it. Haven't you got any sense? It took a long time to get her smiling again. What was it you told her?'

'I just asked her a few questions about Joe Savage,' Tracy said, his eyes narrowing.

'Oh, that's all!' Lou said, coming still nearer until his bulky body blocked out the light coming through the saloon's window. 'You damned fool! Do you know what that girl's been through, moping over him? It took a year to bring her out of it and to get her smiling and laughing again like the old Lucinda. Now you have to come around and start that all up again.'

'It wasn't my intention to — '

'It wasn't your intention! You just thought you'd butt in. You look like another of those damned bounty hunters to me. You sure are acting like one. I'll tell you what your intention is now, mister. Your intention is to get the hell out of Eagle Rock as quick as you can.'

Tracy let the man talk himself out. He thought that after Lou had vented his venom, he would cool down. He was wrong again. Just as Tracy thought the man wasn't going to do it after all, Lou threw a crushing blow with his left fist that landed on Tracy's ear and Tracy staggered away before rolling from the plankwalk into the dusty street, his ear ringing, stars exploding behind his eyes.

Tracy only managed to rise to his knees when Lucinda's huge protector struck again. Looming over Tracy, the big man kicked out viciously at his head. Tracy was alert enough to duck his head to one side and roll away. Lou's boot toe slammed numbingly into his shoulder. As Lou took his stance again, hunched low, fists bunched, Tracy could hear the men behind him cheering the big man on.

'Tear his head off, Lou!'

'Kick him once for me!'

Tracy was barely able to make it to his knees again. Predictably Lou kicked at his head once more. This time, however, Tracy was able to block the man's boot and grab it, ankle and toe. Tracy twisted strongly enough so that Lou was thrown off balance. He spun to the side and then toppled over, cursing as he hit the ground.

Tracy was to his feet first, watching as the panting, cursing big man got to all fours and then pushed himself heavily to his feet.

'You've got this all wrong,' Tracy said, trying to calm the situation, but Lou was having none of it. He plodded toward Tracy as the encouragement from the saloon plankwalk continued. Tracy backed away, then began circling, his fists held in front of him. Lou lunged and Tracy jabbed out with a stiff left hand, catching Lou on the nose.

The punch didn't slow Lou down. He trudged forward, his movements, his panting, bull-like. Tracy hit him with another left hand just over Lou's right eye. Lou swung wildly, missed, and moved closer. Tracy knew he had to keep the bigger man at a distance, and he continued to circle.

He changed tactics slightly. He feinted with his left and as Lou flinched, brought a sharp right hook around. The blow caught Lou on his neck, just below his ear. It must have hurt because Lou paused to wipe at his neck. That lowered his guard enough to allow Tracy to step forward and bring his right arcing in to catch the big man on the hinge of the jaw.

It was enough. Lou's eyes rolled back and he collapsed into the street on his face, unmoving. The angry crowd of onlookers started to surge in Tracy's direction, some still with beer mugs in hand.

'Not tonight, boys,' Tracy said, drawing his Colt revolver from its holster. 'I don't believe I've got any more fist-fighting in me.' The sight of the blue-steel pistol, and the sound of its hammer ratcheting back was enough to convince the others that they wanted no part of this. They backed away in a group, two of them dragging Lou with them toward the Bluebird.

Tracy was trembling. His arm and shoulder ached. He was still a little dizzy, wobbly on his feet, when the drinking crowd had gotten inside the door to the Bluebird Saloon and closed the door. Tracy figured he had had enough. He considered going to the guest house and flopping down on a thin mattress. But he had had enough of Eagle Rock and its citizens for a while.

He holstered his pistol, walked to the stable, and recovered Thunder. Then he swung heavily into the saddle and guided the sorrel out of town and out onto the cold night plains.

7

The night sky was clear, hung with stars so bright that it seemed there were a hundred candelabra suspended there. The moon was a dying presence in the west. Tracy ached; his head throbbed still as he rode east toward the only place he could think of where he might find refuge and a soft bed to sleep on: the Rafter T.

He didn't think Amos Tucker would be upset by his sudden appearance at the ranch. It was early enough in the evening that he would not be disturbing the cattleman. Tracy still believed that Tucker could tell him more about the Joe Savage affair. But not on this night. Tracy was in no mood for a long conversation. He would only show up, apologize for arriving uninvited and ask for a bunk to sleep on. This day had gone on long enough.

When Tracy swung down at the fountain in the Rafter T yard, he was stiff enough that it was labor to do so. The chill night air was beginning to swirl around him as a night wind rose. He made his way to the heavy door through which he had been admitted before and knocked loudly. There was no sound from within. He rapped again and finally heard the faint shuffle of approaching footsteps. He hoped that he hadn't awakened Amos Tucker after all.

The door swung open a few inches and Tracy found himself looking into the eyes of a strange-looking little man. He was dressed in white linen like those a Mexican peon would wear, but this man was not Spanish or Indian. He was shaped like a pear. His red hair was cut in a burr, and the skimpy mustache he wore on his upper lip looked as if it had been newly, roughly sheared.

'I'd like to see Mr Tucker,' Tracy told him. From deep within the house a voice, recognizable as Tucker's, called out.

'Who is it, Jeffrey?'

'Not somebody I know,' the little man said in a strangely accented voice.

'It's Tracy Keyes,' Tracy called over the little man's shoulder. That seemed to irritate him, but Tracy was beyond such petty concerns on this night.

'Tracy? Show him in, Jeffrey!'

Glumly, Jeffrey opened the door wide enough for Tracy to enter. He followed the shuffling Jeffrey across the tiled floor, his boot heels clicking. They found Amos Tucker in the same room Tracy had visited before. There was a fire in the hearth. Not enough to warm the room, but enough to make the chilly night more comfortable for a man sitting near it. Tucker's eyes flickered toward Tracy as he approached.

'Sit down,' Amos Tucker invited, gesturing with a hand. He placed a thick, leather-bound book aside. Tracy was near enough to see that it was a Bible. He seated himself carefully under

Tucker's observant gaze.

'Who was it? Porky Goode again?' Tucker asked with a faint smile.

'No. I made a new friend. I was trying to mind my own business and stay out of trouble. But the men in Eagle Rock don't make that easy.'

'No,' Tucker agreed. 'It's a rough town, and one without enough common sense to go around.' He smiled his gap-toothed smile again. The firelight painted twisting shadows across his broad face. 'What can I do for you, Tracy?'

'Just what you might guess. I need a place to sleep safely tonight. I can't take any more of this rough and tumble right now.'

'No. Well, we can fix you up. I'll have Jeffrey stable up your horse for you, and he can show you where the bunkhouse is. There's only half a dozen men there just now, so there's plenty of room.' The rancher rose to his feet. 'You made up your mind about coming to work for me yet? It's safer than what you're doing.'

It was Tracy's turn to smile, or try to. The expression hurt his mouth. 'I still have to find the answer to the mystery of Joe Savage. I've committed a lot of time and energy to doing that, and I have to see it through.'

'Want to talk to me about what you've been doing?' Tucker asked.

'Not tonight,' Tracy answered. 'I'm not thinking too clearly and I can barely keep my eyes open.'

'All right,' Tucker said, nodding his understanding. Then not too loudly he called out for his man. 'Jeffrey!'

Jeffrey must have been nearby — listening? — for he appeared almost instantly, moving silently across the floor. Tracy glanced at the man's feet and saw that Jeffrey was wearing something that appeared to be felt slippers.

'Jeffrey, Mr Keyes is staying the night. Will you please see that his horse is put up and show him where the bunkhouse is located?'

Jeffrey started immediately toward the door. Tracy followed him after a nod of thanks to Amos Tucker. Outside it was still a clear, starry night, but the wind had increased and there was a chilly edge to it. Tracy took Thunder's reins and led the sorrel through an arch in the back wall of the courtyard, following the silent Jeffrey through the darkness.

The stables were remarkable, as out of place on the wide plains as Amos Tucker's unusual house. They were built of the same material, white-washed adobe. Individual stall entrances were separated by arches. Jeffrey halted in front of the third of these and took the reins from Tracy.

'Want any of your gear?' the house-man asked in his strange accent, which Tracy could still not place. Eastern European? He couldn't even guess.

'Only my rifle.'

Jeffrey nodded, slipped Tracy's Winchester from its scabbard and handed it over. The man led Thunder inside, pausing to light a lantern which hung from the inner front wall. 'I'll see that he's rubbed down and fed,' Jeffrey told Tracy. 'Your accommodations are over there.' He lifted a stubby finger and pointed in the direction of a more usual structure, a long bunkhouse constructed of unbarked logs with a series of slot windows cut into them. A dozen oak trees stood clustered in front of the buildings.

Tracy started that way, pausing to make sure that Jeffrey was going to do his job. He saw the little man working at the cinches of Thunder's saddle. Before continuing on, Tracy looked back again at the big two-story house. He wondered how many bedrooms were incorporated in it, but shrugged off the question. Amos Tucker was already doing him the favor of letting him stay on the Rafter T. A beggar has no right to demand the best of everything. Perhaps Tucker was just protective of his privacy.

Tracy approached the bunkhouse

through the shadows of the oak trees which were now shuddering in the night breeze. A few small brown leaves were shed by the oaks. Tracy walked to the front door of the bunkhouse and entered. Men did not knock on bunkhouse doors out here.

As he entered, he drew a series of hard glances from men playing cards, lying in their bunks, cleaning their guns and doing bits of bridle work. He closed the door behind him and strode stiffly to the nearest man, a dark-eyed, red-faced man who seemed to be in command.

'Mr Tucker sent me over here to bunk up,' Tracy said. He noticed that the card players had suspended their game to watch him suspiciously.

'You a new hire?' the red-faced man asked. There was a touch of salt in his voice.

'Not yet. I'm just spending the night.'

'I don't think we got any spare bunks,' the man said, although looking down the aisle past rows of bunks built for forty men, Tracy saw only six or seven men and twice that many unused beds, their mattresses rolled upon them. Tracy was in no mood for games. He was stiff, sore and cold.

'I'll just see if I can find one,' Tracy answered, his voice now roughening.

'No you won't,' the man with the red face objected, grabbing Tracy's arm as he tried to brush past him, 'not if you're who I think you are. Is your name Savage?'

'No, it isn't,' Tracy said, not amplifying his answer.

'We heard Joe Savage's cousin was going to come out here,' a scrawny blond cowboy on an upper bunk called down. 'What kind of trouble are you planning?'

'None at all,' Tracy said, yanking his arm from the bunkhouse foreman's arm. 'Unless using an empty bed can be considered trouble around here.'

He strode down the aisle, his body still not moving freely. Reaching the last bunk on the right side, he placed his rifle against the wall and untied the strings holding the mattress so that it unrolled on the bunk. There was a thin pillow and a gray blanket inside. They would do. There was a quiet murmuring in the room behind him as he kicked off his boots and crawled into bed, drawing the blanket up to his chin.

After an hour or so as Tracy lay awake, listening to the wind rattling the branches of the oak trees against each other, the lantern was turned down and the bunkhouse fell silent. After another half hour he could hear men approaching his bunk in stocking feet, moving as quiet as Jeffrey in the felt slippers he wore. He slipped his revolver from its holster and waited. When they were within a few yards of his bunk, Tracy threw back his blanket and showed them his Colt.

'Not tonight, boys. I'm not in a playful mood.'

They faded back into the shadows, grumbling and whispering as they crawled into their beds. Tracy waited until they seemed settled again then lay his head back on his pillow. He wondered how they had known that Joe Savage was his cousin. He had told Amos Tucker, of course, but Tracy had thought that he could trust the ranch owner with that information. Then there was Jeffrey to consider. The way the little man slipped silently around that house, he might have overheard them in conversation and spread the news among the cowboys, who obviously held a grudge against Joe Savage. Tracy listened to the sounds of the wind in the trees and later rain spattering against the bunkhouse roof.

He wondered how a man with none but honorable intentions could have made so many enemies in such a short period of time. It was simple, of course: he was riding in the shadow of Joe Savage, a man who would never be forgiven for his crimes. With these thoughts still circling in his head, Tracy gave in to the complaints of his battered body, yawned, and fell finally off into an unclouded sleep.

★ ★ ★

The morning sun was bright and piercing as it beamed through one of the slot windows cut in the log walls of the bunkhouse and into Tracy's face. He turned his head away and cautiously opened his eyes. The bunkhouse was empty except for him. Of course. As had been the case at the guest house in Eagle Rock, these men had jobs to attend to, places to go. They would have risen early and been on their way before or soon after the sun had come up. Tracy carefully sat up, stretching weary legs and battered shoulders, trying to twist the kink out of his neck. He was bruised and sore, but felt better for the night's sleep. He dressed carefully and pulled on his boots slowly, his movements those of an old man.

Picking up his rifle, he walked across the floor to the front of the bunkhouse.

There was a pudgy man in a stained white apron standing there over the iron stove, which warmed the room and provided a surface for cooking.

'Anything left to eat?' Tracy asked. The man raised angry eyes to him.

'If you make it yourself. I'll do nothing for any kin of Joe Savage.' Then he stamped across the room, opened the front door and left, the wind swirling the flaps of his apron around his legs.

Tracy found a loaf of bread and a bread knife and a slice of ham still resting in a black iron skillet. He fashioned a hasty sandwich and went out into the bright morning himself.

What now? he wondered. There seemed little point in visiting Amos Tucker again. Besides, the house was not a safe place to tell secrets. He had no desire to visit Eagle Rock, and it seemed he had already learned all that there was to be learned there. Walking to the stable where Thunder and a contented-appearing Changa waited, he made an impulsive decision — he was going to make his way up to Missionary Ridge and search for Joe Savage's grave himself. If there was one.

The Reverend Cole had told him that he had buried Joe himself and spoken over the grave. Would a Christian man leave his grave unmarked? Tracy didn't know. Maybe, if he was afraid that the bounty hunters would find it and disturb it. Perhaps Joe's grave was what drew Karin Cole to the Mirror Lake property, not the scenery. There was no telling.

Still, it was a place for Tracy to begin his search again. Running around in circles had accomplished nothing except getting himself beaten twice.

The ride to the lake was pleasant enough if Tracy didn't stop to consider the discomfort the bruises his body was carrying caused. The rain had long ago ceased, and only a few white puffball clouds floated aloft on the breeze. He had thought about slipping into his cold weather gear — his buffalo-hide coat

— but after a few miles with the sun rising higher in the east, warming his back, he felt no need for heavier clothing.

He did not know the trail leading to the Missionary Ridge property, but he had been around long enough now to be able to find his way up through the blue-green pines and occasional cedar trees on to higher ground where he could look down and orient himself. He caught the glint of sunlight on water and started down in that direction. He came upon the large square boulder where he had encountered Karin the last time he had visited the region. Almost hopefully, he scanned the surrounding area, hoping to find her at her favorite lookout point.

A foolish hope. He swung down from Thunder, slipped the big sorrel's bit and left it to graze on whatever grass it could find beneath the pines. Standing with hands on hips, Tracy again surveyed the hilltop, more carefully this time. He was looking for some indication of a grave — a marker, a hummock of fresh earth, but there was nothing unusual to be seen.

He tried logic and came up with the same nothing. He thought that Joe must have been buried near the huge gray boulder, but circling it, he saw nothing. He kicked idly at a bundle of litter composed of pine needles, but there was only flat undisturbed earth underneath. Wouldn't Karin have wanted her intended buried near to where she sat on certain days reminiscing? In his mind still there was an image of the copper-haired girl sitting on the rock, knees drawn up, looking dreamily out across the lake.

Looking at . . . ? Tracy decided to walk down to the lake, thinking that it was not the rock which she was seated on, but some unseen landmark which captured her attention. Something she had lost and could never get back. Joe Savage's gravesite might have been what she was mooning over.

He started down the slope, carrying his rifle. This was black bear country and he did not wish to run across one of the fearsome beasts armed only with a handgun. As he walked, his eyes went from point to point, still searching for any indication that the ground had been disturbed. The tall trees thinned and then fell away as he approached the ponds. He noticed rivulets running down the flanks of the hills following the rain. He supposed that Mirror Lake was not always as it now appeared. In the early spring after the snowmelt these narrow rills could become full-grown creeks, filling the ponds until they rose to meet. He could see striated marks on the opposite bank where the lake water had once been much higher than it was now.

All of that was only of casual interest. He had not come to admire or disparage the lake. He only hoped that it led to the grave of Joe Savage.

The Reverend Roger Cole had told Tracy that he had buried Joe 'up on Missionary Ridge' which seemed to indicate higher ground, but might also have been a general location or a deliberate ploy to conceal the exact location of the grave.

Stopping to drink from the icy pond, Tracy felt that he was indeed a fool. This seemed like such a long, pointless journey now. He should have just written the letter he had planned, telling Aunt Enora that unfortunately Joe had passed away, but that he had turned to religion in his last days. Would that be any sort of comfort to the old woman or not? It would beat telling her that Joe had simply disappeared while on some criminal 'adventure'.

Tracy rose to his feet, watching a flight of geese passing overhead in a long 'V', heading to the southern lands. He walked along the riverbank for a little way, seeing the hoofprints of a doe and its two fawns in the sandy soil, and the tracks of a raccoon, but thankfully none of any large predator.

He looked up the pine-clad hill across the lake, at the slope behind him, seeing nothing but the trees gracefully swaying in the wind. Only a knuckle-head would continue his search for the grave of Joe Savage. He cared nothing for the man, never had; he cared nothing about how he had met his end. Yet it was a nagging thing, this mental maze he had entered. For reasons beyond description he felt the strong urging in the back of his mind to continue on until the mystery could be solved and finally put to rest.

An hour or so spent wandering the lower ground turned up nothing. He was beginning to doubt that there was a grave. At least, it seemed, any hope of ever finding it was futile. He started up the path toward the square boulder once more, his battered body complaining of its rough usage. Three strides this side of the forest verge, the first rifle shot from the opposite slope echoed across the lake and Tracy stumbled, feeling the sharp jolt of lead angrily meeting the flesh of his leg.

8

Tracy rushed toward the forest verge in an awkward, stumbling run as the rifleman opened up again. Was it one man or more? A good man with a Winchester can burn lead through his rifle barrel as fast as he can flick the lever, but he thought there were two men firing. One of them was a better shot. Some of the bullets kicked up dust at his feet and chipped the bark of the pine trees near his head while other rounds flew wildly off into the woods.

His first thought was that it must have been Jack Warren and his little pal, Porky, doing the shooting. The bounty hunters might have been up there conducting their own search for the grave, and spotting Tracy, decided to be finally finished with the man they viewed as competition. Limping on upslope, winding his way through the pine trees, it occurred to Tracy that these two were only a single possibility.

What of Lou, who saw himself as Lucinda's protector? Could he have developed that large a hatred? Of course, if he thought that Tracy was not through reminding Lucinda of Joe Savage. Lou must have been sheltering a conviction that Lucinda was his woman. Also, he had taken a fair beating from Tracy in front of his friends from the town. The man had a lot of pride. He might not have been able to let that go so easily.

Then there were the men in the bunkhouse at the Rafter T. They had meant to do him harm the night before because of some grudge they held against Joe Savage. Finding out that he was Joe's cousin and probably complicit, some of them could have trailed after him on this morning. Who else . . . ? He was not thinking clearly enough to enumerate them. He stumbled along, dragging his injured leg now as he wove through the trees. He was panting audibly. Hot blood was trickling down his pant leg. He refused to stop and see how bad the wound was. He had to get back to where he had left Thunder.

What if they had figured on that? Someone could be posted at the head of the trail, waiting to level his sights on Tracy and finish things. Panting, leaning against the trunk of a huge pine tree, he braced himself, hoping that the pain in his leg would abate. That was a false hope. It did not cease, but only increased. Tracy threw back his head trying for reviving breaths of cool air. Perspiration trickled from his forehead into his eyes and soaked through his shirt at the neck and chest despite the coolness of the day. He needed help, but there was none to be had.

A gust of wind rattled the boughs of the pine trees, and dead branches and pine cones were shaken free of their moorings to rain down through the forest. Tracy felt that he could run no more.

He could barely walk.

Turning his back to the tree, he

watched the far hill slope, wondering if the hunters had decided to circle the ponds and pursue him. Their rifles had been silent for some time as Tracy, winding his way through the shadows and the pines, tried to make it hard for them to find a target for their guns.

It was as he watched the far hillside that one of the rifles spoke again, the shot going far wide. But the rifleman had marked his own position with his muzzle flash and following wisp of gunsmoke. The shot was long, the position of the gunman uncertain, but Tracy was tired of not fighting back.

He raised his rifle to his shoulder, and bracing the barrel on a low-hanging branch, he adjusted for windage and drop and squeezed off a shot from his .44–40 Winchester. It was a thin chance, but just squeezing the trigger made him feel better.

Amazingly the shot did not go unrewarded. It took long seconds for the bullet to strike, but when it did, it hit some living creature. As his own gunsmoke drifted around him and was carried away on the swift breeze, Tracy heard the distant sound of a man screaming in pain and bellowing at once. Tracy smiled with grim satisfaction and hobbled along the path again, moving as quickly as he could away from the target his own rifle smoke had sketched against the pine-thick slope.

There was no answering shot. Had it been just the one man and his lucky shot gotten him? There was no point in speculating. Staggering along, twice going to his knees, using the trunks of the pines as handholds, Tracy approached the square boulder at the trail's head, his suspicious eyes searching the open area. He saw Thunder across the clearing. The horse's ears pricked, eyes fearful, and, grateful for that much luck, Tracy made his staggering, stumbling way across the clearing toward his horse. His leg was ready to buckle at the knee, from exertion as much as from the bullet. There was enough blood dripping into his boot to let him know that if he did not get to help and soon, he was in danger of bleeding to death on this lonesome ridge, probably within a stone's throw of the grave of Joe Savage.

He staggered on through the dizzy landscape. There was fire in his injured leg. His head hammered with thudding pain. He was dragging his leg now, using each tree he came to for support. His breath came in heavy pants. He was coated with perspiration. As Tracy paused to recapture his breath a crow high in the branches of the pine cawed loudly, mockingly at him, then flew away.

At last he saw the square boulder ahead of him. It seemed to fade in and out of focus. His head was swimming. He thought he saw Thunder hidden away in the trees, but then the image shifted and altered in his mind, and he realized he was only staring at a dead, broken tree. Had Thunder run off? He struggled forward, knowing that if he could make it to his horse he had a chance. If not, he would be found dead in the forest, probably only a picked-over pile of bones. A feast for the wild things.

He stopped, swaying on his feet, and gazed stupidly ahead. The girl sat on the rock, watching back without moving to aid him. She must have been a pain-induced mirage as well. 'Karin —' he tried to say her name, but his throat was so dry he could make only a strangled animal sound. He wiped the cuff of his shirt across his eyes, and when he looked again, she was gone. The mind can play cruel tricks on a needful man.

He stumbled forward, rifle hanging loosely in his hand. He closed his eyes briefly, fighting back the pain, and when he opened them again, she was there, rushing toward him. This was no illusion, for he could scent her perfume above the earthy smells of the pine forest. He felt her touch as she threw her arms around him to keep him from falling.

He was ready to drop anyway, and so he let her turn him around and place him gently on the pine-needle-littered earth.

The woman wore a deep blue jacket with a lacy white blouse under it, and a long matching blue skirt. He was able to recognize her through the blur of his vision.

'Lucinda?'

'It's me,' she replied.

'But how, why . . . ?'

'We'd better talk about that later.' Her lips were pursed, and her eyes showed concern. 'I drove a buckboard up here. Let's see if we can get you into the back of it. I'll tie your horse — that is your horse, isn't it? — on behind.'

'It's my . . . ' was as far as Tracy got with his answer. With Lucinda's assistance he managed to get to his feet again, and on rubbery legs he was helped to a buckboard concealed in the forest not far from where Thunder stood. Tracy had only a vague awareness of being helped up into the wagon bed, of lying back with Lucinda's blue jacket folded under his head for a pillow.

'We'd better get you back to town, quickly,' she said and from the urgency in her voice, Tracy realized how critical his situation was. The entire left leg of his jeans was now soaked in blood. Tracy watched as she tied Thunder on to the rear of the wagon.

'What are you doing up here?' he asked. He felt the wagon shift as Lucinda climbed up onto the bench seat to drive. She was going to tell him to be quiet, but realized that talking to him to keep him alert and awake was probably the better alternative. The wagon jerked into motion and they started down the trail through the thickly clustered pines.

'When you told me that Roger Cole said he had buried Joe up here, I had to know,' she said across her shoulder. The brakes of the buckboard squealed as she tried to keep their speed on the down-grade contained. She continued: 'I never

believed that story. If Joe is dead . . . '
Her voice wavered a little. 'Then he's
likely buried down in Colorado or Kansas.
Somewhere. Because if he had come
back here, he would have come to see
me first, right? But he isn't dead. A
woman knows these things in her heart,'
she said with hopeful logic.

Tracy wanted to respond, but his
pain had wrapped a sort of paralyzing
cocoon around him. He let Lucinda
ramble on. Her voice was far preferable
to the silence of the grave.

'I just had to make sure that that
woman wasn't up here,' Lucinda said
with sharp-edged intonation. 'You know
who I mean — that Karin Cole. The
one who thinks that *our* home site
— mine and Joe's — is hers to build a
chapel on. The little . . . I could cut her
throat! Take anything she ever says to
you with a pound of salt, Tracy.'

Tracy could not answer even had he
anything comforting to say. His eyes
were closed. A soft, enveloping uncon-
sciousness had overtaken his pain and

146

concern with the world's affairs. He slept as the wagon rolled on across the plains toward the accursed town of Eagle Rock.

★　★　★

The morning sun shone brightly through the glass window. Sheer yellow curtains hung beside it. Tracy tried to lift his head, but could not. His leg had been immobilized. Just where was he? How could it be morning again so soon? He let these questions romp through his mind briefly, found no answers, then gave it up and fell asleep again.

It was much later when he awoke again. He could tell by the lack of sunlight through the window — the sun must have been directly overhead by now. He again realized that he did not know where he was. The room was decorated in colors and patterns indicative of a woman's hand. Lucinda? It had to be. She had somehow managed to get him back to Eagle Rock and up to her room in Mona's establishment. Letting his eyes close a little, trying to shut out the throbbing pain in his leg, he heard the door to the room open. The woman stood there in shadows, a tray in her hand.

'Lucinda?' he asked.

'No, it's not Lucinda,' a strange yet familiar voice answered. He watched as the girl in blue jeans swayed across the room and placed the tray down on the bedside table.

'Melanie.'

'I'm surprised you remember my name,' Melanie Douglas said peevishly. 'This is my room you're occupying. Lucinda brought you up in the buckboard and together we managed to bring you up the back stairs. Her room was not available — she had an 'appointment' that night. I couldn't leave you out in the hall, so I offered to let you stay here.'

'You sound like you wish you hadn't,' Tracy said.

'Well, after a while it gets to be a nui-sance having company around, you know.'

'I suppose. How long has it been?' he asked.

'This is the third day,' Melanie said.

'The third . . .' Tracy was astonished.

'Look,' Melanie said, uncovering the food on the tray, 'you have got to eat some of this. I've been trying to keep you alive on the soup I've been spooning into you. Eat!' she ordered. 'It's from Mona's kitchen and every-thing they make there is good.'

And it was, although Tracy's stomach seemed to have shrunken and he could only eat a little of the fried chicken, creamed corn and biscuits with honey the girl had brought. There was also a wedge of cherry pie on a separate dish, but Tracy regretfully left it alone. His mouth wanted it, but his stomach was protesting the shock of solid nourish-ment.

Propped up on a pillow, Tracy asked, 'Doesn't your aunt mind my being here?'

'She doesn't know. Anyway the only objection she would have is that you're not paying your way.'

'That is true, I guess,' Tracy agreed. He was little more than a charity case. Regretfully, he pushed his plate aside. 'Mona is so large,' he commented, 'and you are so thin, if you'll excuse me for noticing. How do you do it?'

'Simple,' Melanie replied as she put the plates back on to the tray. 'I have made it a habit to eat only the food I cook for myself.'

'What, small meals, vegetables and such?'

'Partly,' she said with a slight smile, 'but chiefly it's because I am the worst cook in the world and can hardly stand my own creations.'

'So Lucinda is . . . working now?'

'Do you like her that much?' Melanie asked, her mouth tightening again.

'I owe her a lot — she saved my life.'

'I suppose so,' Melanie said, seeming reluctant to even give Lucinda that. It was more than apparent that she did not like her. She rose. 'Yes. She has another appointment right now.'

'With Lou?' Tracy asked.

'Yes, Lou Saxon. How could you guess that?'

'I haven't been around Eagle Rock long, but long enough to meet the man.'

'Lou won't have a nickel left in his pockets as long as he keeps seeing Lucinda as he is. Why are men such fools?'

Tracy had no short answer for that question. He did remember Lucinda's comment in the Bluebird Saloon: 'He's pretty possessive for a poor man,' when speaking of Lou Saxon.

'Then Lou means nothing at all to Lucinda?'

'Nothing at all, less than nothing, but the poor sap is too stupid to see it. He's just another bookmark — do you know what I mean? — one more fool to help Lucinda kill time while she waits for Joe Savage to return.'

'Do you think he will?' Tracy asked.

'We can only hope not. That man is pure trouble. I think he's probably buzzard bait by now — I hope so.' Her eyes were set and angry. Melanie had obviously seen much roughness in her life here at Mona's, but she held a certain fierce dislike of Joe Savage in her mind. Tracy wondered why.

'Did he ever try to . . . ?'

'There's nothing Joe Savage didn't try. With anyone,' Melanie said harshly.

She turned to slip out of the room. Tracy decided to ask her:

'How is Lou Saxon?'

Melanie looked at him in puzzlement. 'He's fine, for Lou Saxon. What do you mean?'

'I was just thinking . . . wondering if he'd been shot.'

'I'm sure the dirty old slob has been — somewhere, sometime. But not recently, if that's what you're asking me.'

Then the door closed behind her and Melanie was gone, leaving Tracy alone in the shadowed room. Outside, it seemed that dusk must be ready to settle. The sky had darkened considerably.

Well, that was it, then. Lou Saxon had not been the man Tracy had shot up at Mirror Lake. Then who? He yawned and settled down on the bed again without giving the matter any serious thought. His stomach was full, and he was satisfied for the time being. He had a lot of other questions that he had not asked Melanie. He was hopeful that she would come back so that he could try to find some answers.

No, he was just hopeful that she would come back to visit him. The little woman who so seldom smiled or laughed, who was wise beyond her years, strangely fascinated Tracy. Especially when compared to the blowzy, money-chasing women surrounding her at Mona's with their easy chatter and ready smiles.

He tried to stay awake long enough to keep thinking about Melanie — he knew little about her — but the leg wound and the feeling of satisfaction as his meal settled in his stomach, brought his attempt to an end.

He would sleep tonight and think of Melanie tomorrow.

If he lived that long! The thought suddenly rose unbidden from deep in the back of his mind, and Tracy considered: How safe was he here with no one standing watch or guarding the approaches to this room? Injured, unarmed, he was a sitting duck for anyone wishing to kill him. And he knew that someone was out to do just that.

With a massive effort, Tracy rolled onto his side, his leg complaining bitterly, got halfway to his feet and noticed his pistol hanging in its holster on one of the bedposts. He stretched out a bruised arm and slipped the Colt from its sheath.

Checking the loads he grunted and settled back on to the bed, feeling only slightly more secure. The coming night would be dark and full of stalking creatures.

9

Morning was bright and clear seen through the window of Melanie's bedroom. Tracy was tired of being abed. He thought he could make it to his feet on this day and walk reasonably well. He hoped he could. There was much to do and he was tired of sleeping the days away, ashamed of having used Melanie's room for so long. It was probably her only sanctuary from the world and the chaos of Mona's. Melanie had not complained, but then that did not seem to be a part of her make-up. Where had she been forced to sleep?

Tracy had sufficient reason to be out of bed, and none for remaining there. If he *could* get up. He had made it as far as the edge of the mattress where he sat, his legs dangling, when the welcome, surprising entrance of Melanie caused him to halt his efforts.

'What are you doing?' she demanded, adopting a nurse's tone.

'Getting up. It's time.'

'That's just your optimistic opinion,' she said, continuing to speak in a scolding way. 'How far do you think you can make it?'

'Out of the building, at least.'

'What makes you so sure? The last time I looked at your leg, it was still bleeding.'

For some reason the idea of Melanie looking at the wound in his thigh embarrassed him. He wondered, 'Was it you who patched me together, Melanie?'

'I would have, but I don't know a thing about wounds and broken bones. We haven't a doctor in town. There's an old Crow Indian woman we call in when something like this happens — someone is always getting shot in this place. Arguments over a certain girl. Things like that. The Crow woman came over to have a look at you. She cleaned out the wound and then packed it with moss and spiderwebs, and cornflour, I think — I don't know what all — then bound your leg up tightly in white linen.'

'How much did that cost?'

'You owe me five dollars,' Melanie answered.

'I'll see you get it,' Tracy said. 'I can't reach my pants right now.'

'And you shouldn't try for a few more days,' she said.

'There are things I have to do.' After a pause, he asked, 'Where have you been sleeping, Melanie — since I took over your room?'

'Is that what's bothering you?' she asked with surprise. The scolding tone had fallen away. 'It's simple. This is a hotel, you know. I work here. My aunt owns it; I clean up after someone checks out. I always know where there's an empty room I can use. In the mornings I could always slip in here and get what I needed — since you were always asleep.'

'Well, it was still an inconvenience. I

apologize. But, no, that's not the chief reason I'm leaving. I have things to take care of. Tell me,' he asked, patting the mattress beside him for Melanie to sit down, which she declined to do, taking the wooden chair instead. 'Who is in charge of this town? I mean I know you have no lawman, but is there a mayor, a judge, someone I can take a grievance to?'

Her eyebrows lowered in a slight frown. 'Is this about the shooting?'

'Only distantly. I need some information and the town clerk refuses to let me examine the files.'

'You have to talk to George Parker — he's our mayor and our judge.'

Parker? Where had he heard that name? Of course — that was the man who was letting the Reverend Roger Cole hold his services in his house.

'Where can I find Parker?' Tracy asked.

'He has a small office in town if there's any business he has to conduct, otherwise at his house.'

'I'll try the office, if you'll tell me where it is.' Truthfully he didn't know if he was up to a long ride to Parker's house despite the fact that Thunder was an easy-gaited animal. Tracy rubbed the three-day stubble of whiskers on his chin and asked:

'Is there any way to come by a razor?'

'That's easy,' Melanie said, rising from her chair. Her look was not encouraging. Obviously she thought he still belonged in bed. 'There's a little cupboard downstairs where we keep all the items our customers have left behind. There must be six or seven razors in there. I'll look around and bring you a mug, soap and brush and a razor. That must be scratchy — especially on your throat.'

'It is,' Tracy answered. Melanie was peering at him through squinted eyelids. 'What are you thinking?'

'I was just trying to picture you in a beard, Tracy. I don't think I'd care for it. How long does it take to grow one?'

'Depends on the man,' Tracy said.

'Some can grow a fair crop of whiskers in four, five months.' Then he fell into a meditative silence. Melanie looked at him curiously before going out to find him a razor.

A beard. How long did it take to grow a long one? Had it taken Joe Savage over a year to cultivate his? The thought hit him powerfully. He did not know Joe Savage, hadn't seen him since childhood. And he barely knew the Reverend Roger Cole with his long, John Brown beard, but it gave Tracy something to consider.

Lucinda. Would she know Joe Savage even with a long beard, wearing spectacles? Last seen riding in a buggy with his niece, Karin? Tracy was agitated enough to force his way to his feet, using the bedpost as a prop. Who was Karin who had been in love with Joe Savage? Her uncle who swore he had buried Joe Savage up on Missionary Ridge — a grave which could not be found.

Maybe Joe Savage was running his

final 'adventure' right now. Assume the role of a preacher. Declare himself dead, free himself from the unfortunate Lucinda and take up with Karin who was now posing as his niece. It could be that Joe Savage was no longer an outlaw, but a respected member of the community, busy collecting contributions for the chapel he said he intended to build on Missionary Ridge. Which would explain why they couldn't clear the title to the land.

Joe Savage couldn't have transferred the land to himself before he had finished inventing Roger Cole, and Joe Savage, assumed to be dead, could not now will it to Roger Cole. It was a problem, but nothing a good forger couldn't get around.

Especially if the town mayor and judge, the preacher's patron, George Parker was in on it. His word would keep the hall of records closed to snoopy outsiders.

Tracy did not know the man but he doubted Parker knew about any of this.

For one thing he had his position to consider. For another, Joe Savage would know that he had given Parker something that the judge could hold over his head forever.

Tracy's head was spinning with the long, fanciful tale he had been telling himself. Of one thing he was certain — when Karin had introduced the two men, Roger Cole's eyes sheltered behind his spectacles had reflected a recognition of the name Tracy Keyes. Of course, Joe knew the family name even if he had not seen or thought of Tracy in dozens of years. That was no kind of evidence, either, only suspicion. His head was lost in confusion, and Tracy was happy to have his thoughts interrupted by the return of Melanie Douglas bearing soap, mug, and razor.

As Tracy shaved, watching his reflection in the bluish mirror, his thoughts began to sober. He had taken a coincidence or two and formed what might have been false speculation around them. He wished he could get the preacher and Lucinda face to face, but they were unlikely to show up at the same places or events.

Melanie now did sit on the bed, watching him as he shaved, his eyes intent and somehow darkly determined.

'Have you seen those bounty hunters?' Tracy asked Melanie. For he had not forgotten the threat posed by Jack Warren and Porky. What if they somehow had reached a conclusion similar to Tracy's? It seemed unlikely, but after all, they had not been able to find a grave either. They might still be wondering what Joe Savage's cousin was doing in Eagle Rock. The real explanation would sound flimsy to those who made all of their movements based on profit alone.

Those two wanted Joe Savage or his remains badly. They would not have any qualms about murdering Tracy either.

'Who?' Melanie asked. 'Do you mean that one with the long black mustache and the little one who fought with you? Someone said that was their line of

163

work — I wondered if you were a wanted man.'

'Not by the law,' Tracy said, folding the razor and rinsing his face. He wanted to tell her all about his connection with Joe Savage, with his new, almost wild theory about Joe's present whereabouts, but did not. He let his eyes escape her curious gaze as he took his gunbelt from the bedpost, strapped it on, and asked the way to George Parker's office. She explained carefully, adding:

'If you can make it that far.'

'I think I have to,' Tracy said, settling his Stetson on his head. 'If you see Lucinda, tell her I want to talk to her.'

'Oh, I'll see her,' Melanie said in a tight voice. 'In about an hour, I'd guess.'

'Thanks,' Tracy muttered before he managed to shamble to the door and open it. When he left, Melanie was still sitting on the bed, her eyes turned down, her hands clasped together between her knees. He had no idea what the girl was thinking, but it was obvious she was not happy with him. He would consider that when he had the time.

The fresh air was like a slap in the face when he opened the door to the rear stairs and stepped out onto the landing. Cool, harsh, sudden. He glanced skyward. To the north, clouds were gathering. It seemed there was a chance of rain again. The temperature seemed to indicate that it might even snow.

Just what he needed.

Tracy placed both hands on the banister of the staircase and began inching his way down the steps. He needed Thunder; he was not going to make it far on foot. He realized then that he did not know where his horse was. Lucinda had promised to stable Thunder, but at which establishment? He wasn't going to limp around town checking with all of them. Besides, he thought ruefully, he didn't know if he even had the money to pay for

Thunder's three-days' keep.

That caused him to remember that he had not given Melanie back the money she had spent on his medical fees or for the use of the room. As he rounded the corner of the cross-alley, a blast of frigid air caught him full in the face. He staggered on. For the first time since he had begun this crazy quest he found himself missing Texas.

The clouds were creeping in toward Eagle Rock as Tracy made his staggering way along the street. He found himself stopping on every street corner to catch his breath. Businessmen and hooting cowboys passed him. He was standing still in the midst of energetic activity, spent and beaten. It was a depressing thought. He was like an older man among a bunch of frolicking youths.

Looking up, Tracy noticed that he was standing in front of a dry-goods store, still open at this hour, and he went that way. Opening the door, which was immediately slammed shut by the rising wind, he found the clerk.

'I need a cane Have you such a thing?'

'Yes, sir. We have several very fine Malacca canes.'

Tracy told him, 'I don't even know what that is. I just want a stick to prop myself up. Cheapest you have.'

The clerk, seemingly unoffended, went to the back room and returned with a curved-handle cane which seemed to be made of ash. 'This is quite sturdy, sir,' he said, 'though not what you'd call fashionable.'

'I just want it to do the job it was made for,' Tracy said, taking the cane and putting his weight on it.

'You have been newly injured?' the clerk inquired.

'Newly, yes.'

'You'll find the cane is of more use in your other hand,' the clerk said, still inoffensively.

'I'm right-handed,' Tracy muttered, feeling compelled to offer some excuse for his lack of knowledge. 'Habit, you know.'

He walked across the floor of the

store and back, feeling awkward but slightly more supported. He realized that the bruises and scrapes he had suffered had taken a heavier toll on his body than even his leg wound. He had no strength. Nevertheless he had to continue now.

'Can you tell me where George Parker's office is?' he asked the clerk as he paid for the cane.

'One block up the street, on this side. Over the Bluebird Saloon.'

The Bluebird Saloon. Tracy went out into the windy day, feeling that he was traveling in circles no matter what he tried. The rain began to fall as he made his careful way along the street. At first it was only scattered drops which seemed to do little more than settle the dust, but by the time he had reached the Bluebird, it was falling in earnest, a strong wind pushing the silver rain at an angle against the town. A stormy darkness had settled, and the few people still on the streets were scurrying toward shelter.

There was a light on in an upstairs window, and Tracy decided to take the outside stairs rather than pass through the barroom, not knowing who might be there. He did consider that Lucinda was probably in the Bluebird. Melanie said that it was her habit to go to the saloon at this time of the evening, and he still wanted further conversation with Joe Savage's girlfriend.

With the cold wind pressing at his back, boots and cane both slipping on the wooden steps of the stairs, he made his way to the landing, not sure if George Parker was in. He couldn't be certain that it had been Parker's lantern he had seen lighted in the window.

Entering the upstairs hallway, Tracy whipped the rain from his Stetson. He could hear the revel-makers downstairs and even smell stale beer and whiskey from the saloon. Why would Parker have his office here? The answers were probably simple ones. He was located conveniently in the heart of town and the rent would be low.

On the door of the corner room, illuminated by a lamp in the hallway, Tracy saw a sign with gilt letters on it that read, 'Judge Parker — Town Mayor'. He rapped on the door, was summoned by a muffled voice and staggered in like a three-legged steer.

Parker was seated loosely in his spring chair behind a broad, scarred desk. He was in shirt sleeves and had his eyes fixed on the window, where the driving rain could be seen through the fogged glass. The man had silver hair combed straight back, a waxed silver mustache, and piercing blue eyes.

'I'm Tracy Keyes,' Tracy said. The judge's shrewd eyes studied him.

'George Parker.' He extended his hand. 'I don't believe we've met before. I don't recall your name, at any rate.'

'I'm new to Eagle Rock,' Tracy said, finding a chair to sit in. 'Just trying to survive long enough to leave it alive.'

'Oh, you've had trouble with some of our residents?' Parker asked, looking at

Tracy's cane which he now held across his lap.

'Not exactly; I guess you'd call them drifters.'

'Bounty hunters,' the judge clarified.

'How did you know . . . ?' The judge held up a hand and almost allowed his thin mouth to form a smile.

'We've had trouble with that type sporadically, ever since Joe Savage died. Is that the reason you've come here? The bounty hunters?'

'Indirectly,' Tracy replied and he again unfolded the telegram from his mother and handed it over to Judge Parker, who retrieved a pair of spectacles from his desk drawer and read it, not once, but several times.

'I see,' Parker said, handing the telegram back across his desk. 'Your family wants to know what did happen to Joe Savage, and secondarily if he has left any property of value.'

'Secondarily,' Tracy agreed. 'I believe that solving the secondary question is important to discovering the answer to the first: that is, is Joe Savage dead or not?'

'Everyone knows he is,' Judge Parker said.

'Many times what everyone knows has proven to be wrong. The ancient Egyptians figured they had the universe figured out.'

'Ah, a scholar,' Parker said.

'Hardly, but a few things I learned in school have stuck with me. Mostly that when a sentence starts with 'everyone knows', it's usually wrong.'

'Philosophy aside, what can I do for you? I assume you have come here for a reason.'

'I can't get the town clerk to let me see the property records. I need to know who claims to own the property up on Missionary Ridge, and if it was legally transferred.'

'It's pretty generally conceded,' Parker said with a faint smile — Tracy noticed his deliberate evasion of the phrase 'everyone knows' — 'that the property was given to the Reverend Roger Cole by your cousin after he was baptized shortly before his death.'

'Is that what the records show?' Tracy continued doggedly. The last thing he wanted to do at this point was offend the judge, but he had to know.

'We can take a look,' Parker said, rising to take his homburg hat from the pole rack near the door. 'I wouldn't mind seeing those records myself, though it's never been an issue before. Does your family hope to recover the deed to the property?'

'No, sir. My aunt and mother are both of an age when the last thing they would consider would be pulling up roots and relocating to Wyoming, a place they've only heard of. As for me — the property is pretty, but just about useless. You can't run horses or cattle up in that pine country, couldn't farm the land. Myself; I'd have no use for it either. I only want to know who legally owns it. Because, unless I'm badly mistaken, it's still in the name of the original owner, and that would indicate to me that Joe Savage is still alive.'

Parker was frowning. He glanced at his heavy gold pocket watch and replaced it. 'There's a church service at my house tonight. My wife will scold me if I miss it, but I think we have time to examine the property records.'

'Would it be all right if I attended the services?' Tracy asked as the two men went out into the rain. 'Karin Cole did invite me.'

'A lovely girl; yes, certainly it would be fine with me. Another sheep is always welcome into the fold. And I know that Reverend Cole would be happy to greet a new member to his congregation.'

Would he? Not if what Tracy suspected was true: that the Reverend Cole was really Joe Savage in disguise, and his neatly plotted, nearly-perfect 'adventure' was about to be blown sky-high.

Why would Joe resort to this? A man used to thousands of dollars taken in bank raids and stagecoach stick-ups.

Tracy thought he knew. For one thing the territory was crawling with bounty hunters wanting to collect the money on his head. And he was facing a long prison term if he were tracked down by law officers. They did not chase dead men.

He could revive himself, calling himself Roger Cole, and be treated with respect in the best homes, collecting donations for his chapel on Mirror Lake. He could shake free of Lucinda and live openly with his 'niece' Karin. Perhaps it wasn't the best plan Joe Savage could have come up with, but Tracy had to admit that it was clever.

Did Karin know about all of this? She had to. How else could her lover have foxed her into playing the role he intended for her?

So, Joe, a nice new life, a fine woman, no hangman menacing you . . . Tracy almost envied his cousin at that moment.

'Here we are,' Judge Parker said and Tracy glanced at the door to the records office. The same tight-jawed clerk stood behind the counter, but his demeanor transformed immediately as he saw Parker, who was, presumably, his employer.

'Well, hello, Mister Mayor,' the man said with false affability as his gaze passed over Tracy Keyes. 'What can I do for you this afternoon?'

'That acreage up on Missionary Ridge — I need to see the files on it.'

'You mean Joe Savage's property?' the man asked, his heavy eyelids falling a fraction of an inch.

'Exactly. Bring the property registry out and any addenda there might be to the deed, please, Ezekiel.'

'Yes, sir; that's why we're here, to help.'

Judge Parker gave the clerk a believable but perfunctory smile — one politicians always have on hand. 'We can sit over there,' Parker said, nodding toward a table stationed against the opposite wall.

'Just a minute,' Tracy said, peering into the back room of the office. 'I want to make sure nothing is accidentally lost or falls to the floor, as he retrieves the records.'

'You are mistrustful,' Parker said, unsmiling now.

'I have reason to be,' Tracy said. Zeke was stumping back with a heavy, blue-bound volume in his hands. The glance he gave Tracy might have killed a less determined man. Had Zeke been paid to keep the records unavailable? Possibly.

At the small side table the two, Parker and Tracy, sat and opened the blue book. Tracy let Parker do the search of the records. Scanning the page, using his finger, Parker's eyes looked alert and finally puzzled. He flipped the page over, looking for a later addendum, but there was nothing there.

'Well,' he told Tracy at last, 'that property is in the name of Joseph Savage. It was never transferred to Roger Cole.'

'And if Joe Savage is dead?' Tracy prodded. 'Who would fall heir to it?'

'Without a will . . . ' Judge Parker

blinked behind his spectacles. 'The law generally awards title to the nearest living relative. Who would be . . . '

'His mother, Enora Savage.'

'But you said she wouldn't want it.'

'She might like any profit that could be accrued through its sale.'

'I don't think it would bring much on the market, Keyes. As you have said, it's a pretty piece of land, but just about useless. It could take years to sell. I'm going to have to go through my law books before I can make a final determination as to who has legal rights to this property.'

'One thing we do know . . . ' Tracy began, and the judge was already nodding his agreement. Parker said quietly:

'The Reverend Roger Cole doesn't own it.' He drummed his fingers on the table. 'As I have told you, he is holding services at my house tonight. Afterwards, I'll ask him to step aside with me, and I'll explain matters. Perhaps Joe Savage did intend to sign the deed over to his church, but it was never done, and without evidence, nothing can be done to prove a man's intentions.'

'Am I still welcome to attend the service?' Tracy asked, standing.

'Of course! Why wouldn't you be? Perhaps you can help me when the time comes to speak to Reverend Cole.'

'Perhaps I can,' Tracy said. 'Yes, I think maybe I can.'

10

Lucinda was sitting with two men at a table almost in the center of the Bluebird Saloon when Tracy made his way in the door, hobbling on his cane, dripping water. The storm seemed to have settled in. It might rain all night. Tracy did not know the weather patterns in this part of the country, but the constant thick gloom of the low clouds seemed unlikely to disperse any time soon. Now and then a heavy bolt of brilliant lightning challenged the darkness, punctuating the storm's ferocity.

Catching Lucinda's eye across the room, Tracy started towards her. Unfortunately, Lou Saxon was one of the men sitting with Lucinda, which should have been expected. The lanky red-headed man with them was someone Tracy had not seen before in town.

Making his way through the jostle of drinking men, Tracy stopped beside the table. He made it a point not to lock eyes with Lou. Maybe the man had had enough; maybe not. The sight of Tracy walking with a cane seemed to blunt his anger.

'Can I see you for a few minutes?' Tracy asked. Lucinda's eyes narrowed. She glanced at Lou.

'Again?' Lou asked with menace. Lucinda tried to calm him down before any trouble could start. She touched Lou Saxon's forearm lightly and smiled at him.

'Just for a few minutes, Lou,' she said. 'We don't want anything like the excitement we had last time. Please?'

'Go ahead,' Lou grumbled, tossing a hand. Then he got back to discussing something about the storm and rising creeks with his nameless friend. Lucinda led Tracy to the corner of the saloon. There was no empty table there and so they spoke while standing.

'I want you to go to church with me,'

Tracy said. Lucinda burst out with a peal of laughter.

'You what!' she asked, placing her fingertips to her breast. Then, sobering a little, she searched his eyes, saw he was not joking and asked, 'Does it have to do with . . . him?'

'Yes. At least I think so. Tell me, Lucinda, would you know Joe if he was wearing a beard?'

She frowned, not understanding the question. When she answered she was calm and straightforward: 'If he was wearing a beard, a mask, if he had shaved his head, if he was dressed in robes or stark naked, yes! I lived with that man, and loved him for a long time.' She grabbed Tracy's arm. 'You don't mean that you think he is still alive?'

'I do. You're the only one who can prove it.'

'But where has he been? Why . . . ? What do you want me to do, Tracy?'

'Just come along with me out to Judge Parker's house. I want you to meet someone. I know it's a rotten night to be traveling, but I think you should go along.'

'You think you've found Joe,' Lucinda said, her hand dropping away from his arm. 'Of course I'll go. I need to know where he's been, why he hasn't returned to me.' Her voice softened. 'I need to know if he ever meant to come back at all, or if I've been living hopefully on a lie all this time.'

Lucinda added, 'I've got to get rid of Lou so he doesn't get some wild idea. I can rent a buggy at the Royal Stable — that's where I left your horse as well. Three blocks east on the right side of the street.' She was speaking in a rush now, and looking across the saloon, Tracy could see Lou Saxon's jealous eyes fixed coldly on them.

'Half an hour,' she said, turning away. She had not failed to notice the cane he was using. 'Are you up to it, Tracy?'

'If you are,' he replied.

Tracy hobbled out of the saloon, taking the long way around Lou

183

Saxon's table. He doubted that the cane he was using would bring any mercy toward him. No, Tracy would have to shoot Lou Saxon this time if he made a move, and that would cancel the evening's plan.

Tracy hadn't told Lucinda all of the facts, about why they were going to the church service — likely for the first time in Lucinda's short, madcap life. He hadn't wanted to prejudice her reaction upon meeting Roger Cole. She must have been wondering; maybe she had even figured it out, but Tracy hadn't told her.

He realized that another reason he had not revealed what he thought he knew was because it could all be a pipe dream, a group of unrelated facts selected out of some brain fever while he lay ill and forced them to fit together. Because he wanted them to fit!

Because Tracy was tired of all of this — of Joe Savage, Lou Saxon, Jack Warren and Porky, Mirror Lake and Eagle Rock. Standing under the awning of the Bluebird Saloon he again longed for Texas. True, he had nothing waiting for him there, but life had seemed much simpler, safer on the old Double M Ranch.

It did no good to think of those Texas days now. He started on toward the Royal Stable while the high wind sent the silver rain angling down, pelting the awnings, obscuring even the nearest of buildings until they were only dark, haunting shadows. Was there anyone out there watching, waiting for him? There was no telling, and so Tracy slogged steadily on. Each time he had to step down from the plankwalks, he was forced to wade through deep mud. The ferrule of his cane sunk into the muck with each step, it proving to be more of a hindrance than a help under these conditions.

He finally saw the Royal Stable opposite, and he waded through mud and standing water to reach it. Inside, it was dry, but little warmer, even though the plank walls cut the wind. Familiar smells: hay, horse droppings, carbolic and heated animal flesh. And a familiar face. Thunder had his head up and was watching Tracy's arrival over the stall partition. There was a hint of reproach in the big sorrel's eyes. The animal just didn't like to be left alone while its owner went off on wild human endeavors.

The stablehand in muddy boots and blue overalls came in through a side door wiping his hands on his clothing. Tracy was stroking Thunder's muzzle.

'Your horse?' the man asked gruffly.

'It is. Lucinda brought it in for me — I had a little trouble,' he said gesturing toward his injured leg and cane.

'That's fine. I just wanted to make sure you was the right gentleman. Are you taking him out on a night like this?'

'It's no night for riding, is it?' Tracy said as a distant boom of thunder sounded. 'But, yes, I guess I'll be taking the sorrel.'

186

The stablehand eyed Tracy doubtfully. 'Are you sure you can even get aboard?'

'I'll be all right if I use a right-side mount. He'll allow it.' Most horses were used only to a left-side mount, that being the way they were trained, a custom that went back to old Europe when a man with his sword usually hung on the left side found it difficult to mount from the right side, the weapon dangling in the way. But Tracy had long noted that an Indian pony ridden bareback could be mounted by its owner from the left, from the right, with a leap from the rear without objection from the animal, and five years ago when he had first purchased Thunder he had trained him to allow a mount from either side. Why adhere to an outdated custom?

But there was a point to the stablehand's concern. Could Tracy even mount at all, using his good right leg for leverage? Right then Tracy couldn't have said. He quit thinking about it; the question might never arise. He just knew he would feel somewhat more secure having Thunder with him.

'Lucinda wants the buggy she used a few days ago, the one with the canopied top.'

'Her regular buggy?'

'I suppose it is. I don't know her that well. One that'll keep the rain out of her face.'

'Mister,' the stablehand said, 'they don't make any such thing. Not for a night like this.'

After that the man fell into grumbling and slow cursing. Tracy realized that he had forced the man to go out in the rain again to find a team of horses, harness them, and hitch them to the buggy. In other times he might have offered to help, but just now his body wasn't up to it. He found Thunder's reins and bit hanging on a provided nail in the stall, and his blanket and saddle on the partition. For a chore which he performed almost daily, the saddling and outfitting of the horse was challenging and uncomfortable in the extreme. His shoulders seemed to have no strength in them; his ribs were bruised, and his leg was on fire.

He knew now who had shot him out at Missionary Ridge, who it had to be: Joe Savage. There had been no other interested parties in the vicinity. And who had Tracy nicked out there? Joe or some hired flunky? He would see once they got to the services at the Parker house.

This was going to make an interesting letter to his mother, Tracy thought with a bitter smile, and a nice gift to Aunt Enora who was a fidgety, sincere, perpetually worried old woman who sincerely loved her son. Well, he considered, it was Joe Savage's doing — all of it — and not his own.

Tracy led Thunder out of his stall, found an empty horseshoe nail keg near the front door and sat down on it, listening to the rush and grumble of the storm outside. The stableman came back in within half an hour, leading the rain-slick team of horses and the buggy with the folding canvas top. He shot a scowl at Tracy, brushed water off himself and toweled off the horses. Lucinda had not come.

Fifteen minutes later she still had not arrived and now it was true dark outside, the sun having slipped away behind the screen of the dark storm clouds. The shops had closed down; the townspeople were sheltered in their homes. Undoubtedly the saloons were still going at a rousing pace, but few men would be coming in, fewer going out into the rain, having found a place to ride out the storm. A lot of whiskey would be sold on this night.

Had Lou used force to prevent Lucinda from leaving the Bluebird? Tracy doubted it. He saw himself as Lucinda's protector, but he was more like a neglected yard dog who approached, placed a paw on her knee, and hoped only for a pat on the head.

Besides, Lucinda was quite popular

around town and Tracy doubted that other men would stand for any rough stuff.

Where could she be? For one of the few times in his life Tracy wished he had bought himself a watch. They might have been a necessity for town folks, but there was little need for such a device out on the plains.

Another half an hour crept past. The stablehand was obviously growing irritated. Tracy avoided meeting his eyes. Even Thunder seemed annoyed as time went by. The sorrel stamped his stockinged right front foot on the ground and eased forward, trying to nuzzle Tracy into motion.

At last Lucinda appeared out of the rain, a trembling creature wearing a long, hooded, dark blue cape. She carried a dark blue purse with wooden handles resembling a small carpetbag.

'I had the devil's own time getting away from Lou,' she said. 'I kept offering excuses and he told me that it was raining hard and I'd get sick.

Finally I just slipped out of the kitchen door into the alley. I had to go back to my room to get this,' she said, sweeping her hands down along the blue cape. 'Lou was right about one thing — I was risking pneumonia the way I was dressed.'

'Well, you're here now. Are you ready to go?'

'I suppose. But, Tracy, this is still all a little mysterious.'

'I know. Do you know the way to Judge Parker's house?'

'Of course. Everyone does. Some people ride out there on Sundays just to take a look at it. It's a big place.'

'What do we do about . . . ?' Tracy asked the stable-hand who was trans-fixed by Lucinda's presence. It couldn't have been often that he had a pretty woman in his stable.

'Lucinda can pay for the use of the buggy and team when she brings them back, same as always. You — I don't know you — you owe me for three days' care of the sorrel.'

Lucinda was opening her large purse, but Tracy placed his hand on hers. 'I think I've got it,' he said, digging deep into his pockets. She was a funny girl, Tracy thought. Promiscuous, but faithful in her own way. Generous, and kind to him when he was injured. He didn't try to figure her out just then. She was just another prisoner of her time and of this wild country.

It took about three seconds of consideration before Tracy decided he should clamber into the buggy with Lucinda, and tie Thunder up behind rather than trying to ride the sorrel through the whip of the wind and the down-pouring rain. It was growing much colder, too, as the storm lingered. For the first time he wished he had his buffalo coat with him, but it was stored with his saddle-bags in Melanie's room at Mona's place.

Tracy rode on through the driving rain in the buggy, watching Lucinda's surprisingly deft handling of the reins of the two-horse team. He saw that she was shivering beneath her cloak. He himself was shuddering with the cold. He took comfort from the idea that Judge Parker's house could not be that far distant from town.

Lightning flashed and illuminated the muddy road clearly. He and Lucinda did not attempt to speak. The canvas roof of the buggy was pelted with drops as hard and swift as buckshot. For that much Tracy was grateful as the determined saloon girl drove on. There was nothing left to say to her at this point, and he had no answers to provide to her questions.

It loomed up behind the dark, shuddering ranks of an oak grove as lightning struck again, quite nearby: A vast, yellow-brick house of two stories with rows of carriages parked in front of it. The house was even larger than Amos Tucker's pseudo-Spanish home. There were three chimneys that Tracy could see: One at either end of the house, and another nearly in the center which must have been where the main living area was. Smoke rose from each of these, spiraled upward, and was whipped away by the gusting wind. Lucinda spoke through chattering teeth:

'Well, at least it will be warm inside.'

It would be that, and if Tracy was right, it might also heat up rapidly.

There was a man with a black slicker and matching hat standing miserably on the porch when they arrived and he came out to take the reins to the horses. That was more refinement than either Lucinda or Tracy had ever encountered in the West. Tracy slipped from the buggy and looked up at the long yellow house. Judge Parker certainly had a lot of money, no matter how he had come by it. That did not matter to Tracy just then, and probably never would. He and Lucinda mounted the brick steps to the front porch. Lucinda threw back the hood of her cape, smiled at Tracy, and asked, 'Are we ready to go in?'

'I don't know, but it's time,' he answered, lifting the heavy ornate brass knocker on the white-painted door to rap for admittance.

Expecting a servant, Tracy was surprised when Judge Parker himself opened the door to the brightly lit house. He reached out and shook Tracy Keyes's hand.

'I'm glad you could make it,' the judge said. He was wearing a brown suit with a black bolo tie, his hair, as ever, well-barbered and groomed. He peered tightly through the lenses of his spectacles at Lucinda. 'And you've brought a guest. Do we know each other?'

Lucinda said, 'Everyone knows you, Mayor Parker.' Her smile was brilliant. 'And you might remember me. You fined me fifty dollars last month.'

'I see,' Parker said. Creases of concern furrowed his forehead. He obviously didn't want anything to ruin this evening or his standing in the community. They crossed the foyer, Lucinda handing her cape to a girl-in-waiting, but keeping her purse, and entered the living room, set up with extra chairs on this night to face an elevated stage to the rear. There was an oak lectern on this, obviously intended for the Reverend Roger Cole. They were offered wine, which both refused, and introduced to a stout, gray-haired woman who was Mrs Parker. The older lady eyed Lucinda's deep-blue satin dress, appraising her correctly with that single glance.

Parker whispered something to her, probably about the fallen most needing religious guidance, and both turned away with equally false smiles.

'Let's find seats,' Tracy suggested. Other men in evening dress and ladies in their finery still milled around, sipping at a pale wine in crystal glasses. Tracy caught a glimpse of Amos Tucker across the room, but their glances never met.

Tracy and Lucinda sat in the third row, on the aisle. There must have been some signal given, for after a few more minutes the general conversation died down and others began searching for seats. Potential contributors to the chapel Reverend Cole intended to build? They certainly seemed to be comfortable in their wealth. The men wore tailor-made suits; the women's jewels sparkled in the light cast from the huge fireplace.

As the assemblage settled into their seats, the edge of the dark rear curtain parted and Tracy saw Karin Cole peering out. Then the curtain edge dropped again and Judge Parker mounted the jury-rigged stage to welcome his friends and offer the usual remarks such occasions engender. Parker rambled on for five minutes or so, his speech sounding more like an election campaign talk than anything else.

Finally, with a flourish of his arm he summoned the guests of honor from behind the curtain. Roger Cole, looking solemn, came out onto the stage holding hands with Karin, who was obviously nervous. The two had a lot riding on this event.

Beside him Tracy saw Lucinda from the corner of his eye. She was leaning forward intently, eyes narrowed. Her right hand was inside her capacious bag. She muttered something that Tracy did not catch.

Roger Cole was speaking at the lectern now. 'As Saint Paul said in Timothy II — '

'You son of a bitch!' Lucinda yelled at the top of her lungs, getting to her feet. In her hand was a big blue-steel Colt .44 revolver. Before Tracy could grab her arm, she had fired it twice, the reports deafening in the confines of the room. Acrid smoke rolled toward the ceiling.

Lucinda's first shot had hit nothing, slamming into the plaster wall behind the curtain. The second caught flesh. Karin had leaped in front of Roger Cole at the sound of the first shot, and Lucinda's bullet, intended for Roger, had caught her in the back, just below her neck. Her hands slid away from the preacher as she slid toward the floor.

In the front row, an older woman shrieked and fainted dead away. Men rushed toward Lucinda, but Tracy had already wrested the pistol away. She shrank back into her chair, her hands covering her face.

Joe Savage was gone.

11

In the excitement, Joe Savage had fled, leaving Karin wounded and possibly dying on the stage. The men present had been more concerned with seeing to Karin and restraining Lucinda, than in pursuing Savage. Well, why wouldn't they be? They still had no idea of the preacher's former identity.

Tracy, on the other hand, had just had his suspicions confirmed, although not in the way he would have preferred. Lucinda looked up at him once, seemed ready to faint herself, and was taken away by Judge Parker and three other men. The rest of the room was in an uproar, people pointing, shouting, women sobbing.

Tracy hurried, if his shuffling gait could be called that, toward the front door, wielding his cane clumsily. Joe had exited the house. Of that he was sure. Why would the man hang around knowing that the game was up?

Now — how to find him?

The cold rain was driving down. The night was dark as sin. Tracy slogged and slipped his way toward the nearby white barn to find Thunder. The man who had taken their animals was nowhere around.

Tracy burst into the barn, almost falling again, and found the sorrel. He had guessed that the hostler, an employee of Parker's, would not bother to unsaddle the horses, which were to be kept there only for the short duration of the service, and he was right. Nevertheless he checked the cinches on his saddle, found that they had been loosened, and strapped them tightly again.

As Tracy swung clumsily aboard from the right side, Thunder tossed his head in aggravation, but he stood for it. Throwing his cane aside, Tracy heeled Thunder into motion and rode out of the closed barn into the swirl and menace of the storm.

There was not a star to be seen, no shadow of a fleeing man. Which way? It was too wild outside for Joe to risk having to camp out on this blustery night; he could not go into Eagle Rock where they wanted his head on a platter. The empty land left Joe with few choices. Tracy, knowing that he was probably not thinking clearly, believed that Joe, being a creature of habit, as all men are, would head for a region he knew well, where he felt safe: Missionary Ridge and Mirror Lake.

It was certain that Joe knew the area better than any man, might know of hidden trails, perhaps lake caves where he could shelter against the night and plan his next move. Tracy was determined to make sure there were no more plans for Joe Savage.

Joe's time must run out. Tonight.

Joe Savage was poison to everyone he met or involved in his schemes, to family and strangers alike. Riding out only on a hunch, Tracy guided Thunder toward the high ground, which he knew not as well as Joe Savage, but well enough by now to make his way up along the pine-clad slopes toward Missionary Ridge as the rain pelted down and the cold wind blew, gusting through the trees.

Once he thought he saw the hoof prints of a horse in the muddy earth, but it was too dark to be sure. Then he was into the pines, weaving his way upward. The trees did little to abate the drive of the rain. At times the rain turned to sleet, and after a few minutes he saw snow beginning to collect on the rugged trees. He again cursed himself for not bringing his buffalo coat along. The man who had advised him to buy one had known what he was talking about.

Tracy crested out the ridge not far from the square boulder where he had first seen Karin. He paused to let Thunder blow, considering. What made him so sure that he could catch and capture Joe Savage, a man who knew the area intimately and was known to be a swift gunhand, and not shy about using his skills?

And if Joe Savage had decided to proceed on foot, how could a crippled man keep up with him or find him in the swirl and rush of the storm? That would be impossible — Tracy decided to go with the theory that a western man does not abandon his horse except in extreme emergencies. And even if he knew that his cousin was tracking him, Tracy doubted that the confident outlaw would consider his situation dire. Joe held all of the high cards.

In the silence of the darkness and the now-falling snow, Tracy made his way down the slope, winding through the pine forest, his Winchester rifle in his hand.

He paused again near the square boulder, listening for some sound that could be heard above the whistle and roar of the storm — a horse nickering, a striking steel-shod shoe against a rock in passing. There was nothing to be heard in the dark night except for the unrelenting storm. Which way now? The pursuit seemed a futile endeavor. Tracy squinted against the wind and snow and started Thunder slowly down the slope toward Mirror Lake.

He had not made it a hundred feet when a shot rang out near at hand and Tracy bailed out of leather. Stupidly, out of habit, he had taken the left side and his leg was instantly shot through with violent pain. *Stupid*, he told himself as he crumpled against the ground, trying to hold on to Thunder's reins and his Winchester at the same time.

In the end he lost both of them. Thunder snapped his head up and bolted away. The Winchester was lost to the night. Tracy's leg felt as if a hundred poisonous vipers had struck it. He managed to sit down at the base of a massive pine tree and free his Colt from its holster. He had failed; he was going no further, he knew. He sat with his hatless head thrown back, gulping for air, as sleet and snow drove down out of the black skies. For a moment the wind ceased and Tracy was able to make out the half-moon skulking past the bandit clouds, lighting their fringes with an eerie silver light.

The shadow disconnected itself from the night gloom and came slowly forward, like a stalking wolf. Joe Savage had lost or discarded his unneeded spectacles. His long beard was dank and tangled. There was snow on the shoulders of his coat and fiery hatred in his eyes. The pistol in his hand was cold and steady.

'Why?' he asked Tracy as he approached, his boots soundless on the pine needles underfoot. 'Why did you have to come all this way and poke your nose into my business? I had a good thing going. A beautiful woman, all the comfort of my new friends and money coming in — legally gained money. What could cause you to ride all this way and destroy my life?'

'Your mother wrote and asked me to

see if you were all right. Dead or alive.'

'What kind of fool would travel this far to satisfy an old woman's whim?' Joe demanded in a sneering voice.

'My kind, I suppose,' Tracy said quietly. He now saw the look in Joe Savage's eyes that they had held the day that he had wanted to crack his cousin's skull with a stone, all those years ago. Joe had not inquired about Karin. Perhaps she was only a symbol of status to him, a bedmate necessary only to complete his charade. Tracy doubted that Joe had ever cared about another human being in his entire life.

'What do you mean to do now?' Tracy asked as the howling wind recaptured its strength.

'What else is there to do?' Joe shrugged. 'I'll have to plan out a new adventure — though how I'm going to find something as soft as this one was, I don't know.'

'What about Lucinda?' Tracy asked through his pain.

'What about her?' Joe shot back.

'She's just a woman. If you haven't noticed, the world is full of them. As far as I'm concerned, she can go to hell, as can you, Tracy Keyes!'

Joe's eyes still held that look — the one from long ago when he had held a rock in his hand over Tracy's head. For a moment the two images merged in his mind; Tracy rolled his head away to avoid the rock and a .44 slug from Joe Savage's pistol slammed into the pine tree beside Tracy's head, spattering his face and neck with bark.

Tracy Keyes raised his pistol and fired into Joe Savage's body. He hit him twice, although the second shot proved unnecessary as lead punctured Joe's breast and ribcage, stopping his life instantly as the bullet spun into his heart.

Tracy sat shuddering in the night, staring at the still form collapsed against the cold earth. He wanted to ride, to run away from the sight, but he could not muster the strength. He rested against the pine as the snow fell in blankets, forming a white grave which obliterated the cooling flesh of Joe Savage beneath it.

It must have been an hour later, when the storm seemed to have broken, that Tracy awoke with his eyelids frosted, his leg numb and yet fiery with pain. He tried to move his lips, and whistled up Thunder, who had returned like a faithful dog to find its master. Tracy clasped the sorrel's reins and commanded the big horse to back up. With those and the tree beside him as support, Tracy managed to get to his feet, throw his arms around Thunder's neck, and slowly, painfully, climb into the saddle from the right side.

He started Thunder and rode on through the darkness and the cold of night, unsure of his way, wondering how long this madness could continue.

★   ★   ★

The room was warm after the brutal chill of the night. He knew the room but couldn't recall how he had come to be there again. It belonged to Melanie, that much he knew. Her scent even lingered there, on the pillows, in the air.

There was some loud bantering along the hallway and clomping boots tramped past — men feeling much better than Tracy was at that moment. The light streaming in the window told him that morning had already arrived. He sat up in bed, not seriously wounded again, but suffering from the accumulation of aches, pains, and bruises he had suffered in this unlucky town. It was time he was up and moving again. He was not going to spend another three days abed.

He had a clear memory of everything that had gone on the night before up until the time he had passed out, clinging to Thunder's neck. Presumably he had made it back to town, or near enough so that someone could salvage him once again.

As he was pulling on his boots the

door opened and Melanie entered, smiling ruefully. 'You are the darndest man for getting into trouble,' she said, only half joking.

'It had to be finished,' Tracy replied, sagging now on to the bedside chair. He told her an abbreviated but fairly complete version of what had occurred the night before.

'And so you ended up killing your own cousin? That couldn't have felt good.'

'No,' Tracy said, 'but it didn't feel all that bad either, considering the alternative.' He pondered for a moment, studying the dust motes dancing in the sun's rays falling through the window. 'But I should have been more careful in my planning. I don't know if Karin Cole survived or not, but they'll have to bring Lucinda up on attempted murder charges at the least.'

'Karin didn't make it,' Melanie said, her eyes turned down. 'The news is all over town this morning.'

'So in the end I didn't do Lucinda

any favor, did I?'

'You didn't cause it.'

'No, I guess not. Where have they locked her up?'

'She's right down the hall in her own room, loosely guarded,' Melanie told him.

'You know this town — would they hang her?' Tracy asked anxiously. Melanie laughed.

'Not in Eagle Rock! They'd sooner hang Judge Parker if he suggested it. Under the circumstances, I don't see that they can even call it attempted murder. Accidental death — Karin jumped into the way, didn't she?' Tracy nodded and Melanie went on. 'They can't get Lucinda for shooting at Joe Savage — a wanted man — any more than they could charge you.'

'I hope you're right,' Tracy said glumly.

'I'm right. Lucinda has too many friends in this town to be convicted of something like that. You might not have many friends, but you were forced to shoot down a wanted criminal. That's not a crime in this territory.'

'I know,' Tracy said, rising to his feet. 'You've made me feel better about things, Melanie. Tell me, can Lucinda have visitors? I'd like to see her.'

'It's still like that, is it?' Melanie said. Perplexed, Tracy told her:

'It's not still like that. It was never like that. I thought you knew. I happen to like the lady, that's all, and I got her into a lot of trouble.'

'She's in her room,' Melanie said, and she spun away and walked out of the room, her face unreadable, her eyes nearly closed. Tracy didn't get it, but he shrugged off his concern.

There was a man tilted back in a wooden chair beside Lucinda's door. Her guard, Tracy supposed. Tracy asked him:

'OK to visit?'

The guard just gestured widely with his arm and so Tracy rapped, was summoned and went in. Lucinda sat at a tufted chair in front of her mirrored dresser, brushing her glossy dark hair. She said, 'Well, I see you made it again.'

'Do you know how I got here?'

'Sure I do. On the way back from Judge Parker's house we saw your horse standing beside a hummock of snow. We picked you up and placed you in the back of the buggy. When we got to town, Parker asked where you belonged and I told them to carry you up to Melanie's room.'

'She didn't mind?'

'Mind?' Lucinda smiled. 'You really don't know much about women, do you?'

'I suppose not, but I had already forced her out of her bed for three nights.'

'And she didn't complain then, either, did she?'

'No,' Tracy said thoughtfully, 'she didn't.'

'Well, then,' Lucinda said with a smile, as if that explained everything.

'None of that meant anything,' he protested.

'Maybe not to you, but it might have

to Melanie, you know.'

Tracy hadn't come to talk about himself. He changed the subject.

'What did Judge Parker tell you? About what the charges against you might be, Lucinda?'

'Along the road I told him what you had found out about Roger Cole being Joe Savage, about how furious I was when I saw through his disguise, how I just lost my head. By the time we reached Eagle Rock he said I was looking at a term for negligent homicide or maybe manslaughter, possibly reduced to accidental discharge of a firearm resulting in death. He said he'd have to dig into his law books, having never come across a case exactly like this one.'

'Sounds like he's going to go easy on you.'

'He was talking about supervised probation, meaning I couldn't leave Eagle Rock.' Lucinda sighed and put her hairbrush down. 'Where would I go, anyway?'

'No ambitions?' Tracy asked.

'My ambitions are dead,' she said sincerely, rising to rest her hands on Tracy's shoulders. 'Don't take that to mean that I'm angry with you. I'm angry with Joe Savage, though to hold a grudge against a dead man seems pretty futile, doesn't it.' She sagged onto the edge of her bed and looked down briefly, then again up at Tracy. 'Joe Savage was the only man I ever loved, honestly. When I saw him, I felt that the whole world had betrayed me. I'll never get over him, but he just doesn't matter anymore outside of being a lesson learned.'

'I don't know how that must feel. Can you get out of this room, to go to eat, for example?'

'Yes, that's what I'm getting ready for, as a matter of fact. So long as my guard goes along I can do mostly whatever I want until the trial.'

'Need some breakfast company?' Tracy asked.

'No.' Lucinda shook her head. 'I've got an escort. Lou Saxon. You know, Tracy, he isn't really that bad, as men go.'

12

There was a still, peaceful feeling in the air. The sky was brittle and cool, but no wind stirred the long pines. Earlier, Tracy had seen a family of deer with a spotted fawn, struggling to walk on its spindly young legs, down along the lake. The run-off from the fall rains and the new snow-melt, announcing the coming of spring, had filled the basin where the deer drank.

Riding Thunder back toward the log house on the ridge, he saw that his other horse, Changa, was tethered there. She did not so much as glance Tracy's way. The little white mare stood hip-shot and lazy, grateful that her long-riding days were gone. As was Tracy.

He had written to his mother and Aunt Enora, not lying but omitting a lot about Joe Savage. Yes, he was dead, but he had been attending church services the very night he passed away, so he supposed the next decision was God's. There was no point in relating the manner in which Joe had died. What would be the point in upsetting the old women? Enora could make what she wished of his report.

He had told her of the property on Missionary Ridge and promised to send the legal papers to her when Judge Parker had finished examining them. Two months later, Tracy received a reply from Enora saying that she had no use for property in faraway Wyoming and that he had performed a service for her which had certainly involved a lot of time, expense, and probably hardship. She was grateful to him, she said, and if he had any use for the property, or could sell it, he was welcome to it. There was also a separate notarized quit-claim document leaving the land to her nephew, Tracy Keyes. Tracy handed that over to the judge as well.

Within a week — the same week that

Parker ruled the shooting of Karin Cole by Lucinda was accidental — the judge summoned Tracy to the county records office where the dour Ezekiel dutifully added the transfer of ownership papers to the land files.

'You're a taxpayer now, Tracy,' Judge Parker had said, smiling.

'I guess I am, though I don't know if I'll be able to keep the payments up.'

'Of course you will,' Parker said in a friendly voice. 'Once the bounties on Joe Savage started coming in, I filed for payment on your behalf. I hope that was all right — of course, you'll have to pay me something for my work. The Wells-Fargo stage company alone had a five-thousand dollar reward on his head. There will be others, of course. Joe Savage was not an unknown man in this territory.'

'No, I guess not,' Tracy said a little gloomily. Well, he was off to a good start and already wealthier than he could have hoped to ever be down in Texas. On his way out of town he saw

Lucinda and Lou Saxon riding in her buggy. Lucinda waved cheerily and Lou lifted a grudging hand.

Jack Warren and Porky had long since left Eagle Rock on the trail of their next prey, probably still imagining that Tracy had somehow cheated them out of a bounty that was their just due.

Tracy had pondered the problem of what to do with the Missionary Ridge property for some time. He had no money, and so he had gone to work for Amos Tucker out at the Rafter T for a while. The hands there were still not friendly toward him, but they accepted him and let him do his work without harassment.

When the first bounty money from Wells-Fargo came in, Tracy immediately put it in the bank and again rode out to Missionary Ridge. It was as it always had been: a pretty parcel of limited use. Tracy made his decision then and rode back to Eagle Rock to tie the loose ends together.

There wasn't much on the ridge

except for an abundance of timber, and Tracy got to work harvesting some of it. He had been working four days a week on the Rafter T and three days on slowly building his own log house on the ridge. Amos Tucker didn't complain about the arrangement. Tracy was doing his job on the ranch and Tucker was still losing cowhands to Montana and had made up his mind not to rehire any who came drifting back from the northlands.

Now the log house was completed. Smoke drifted lazily into the air from its chimney. Thunder was ready to go to work; he preferred herding cattle to standing idly as Changa did. Tracy patted the big sorrel's neck. He was in no rush to ride out to the Rafter T— it was not one of his regular work days — but one of the mares out there had given birth to twin foals and he felt obligated to check on them.

He tied Thunder next to Changa. Thunder tried to nuzzle her, but she ignored him. She had long ago signaled her indifference to the sorrel, but Thunder kept trying. For a long minute Tracy stood looking out across the pine-clad land, his land, at the lake now swollen with clean water from the snow-melt. On this still morning it gleamed like a mirror set between the two rising ridges. He enjoyed the view for a time and then turned and tramped into the cabin where Melanie was busy cooking their breakfast.

THE END

We do hope that you have enjoyed reading this large print book.

Did you know that all of our titles are available for purchase?

We publish a wide range of high quality large print books including:
Romances, Mysteries, Classics
General Fiction
Non Fiction and Westerns

Special interest titles available in large print are:
The Little Oxford Dictionary
Music Book, Song Book
Hymn Book, Service Book

Also available from us courtesy of Oxford University Press:
Young Readers' Dictionary
(large print edition)
Young Readers' Thesaurus
(large print edition)

For further information or a free brochure, please contact us at:
Ulverscroft Large Print Books Ltd.,
The Green, Bradgate Road, Anstey,
Leicester, LE7 7FU, England.
Tel: (00 44) 0116 236 4325
Fax: (00 44) 0116 234 0205

*Other titles in the
Linford Western Library:*

NINE DEAD MEN

Walter L. Bryant

Ten years after his life is saved, Jason drifts into Inspiration. He believes fate has given him an opportunity to repay the debt when he hears of the leader of an outlaw gang, Adam One-ear. But his determination to meet Adam is complicated by the intervention of a sheriff who wants to kill the outlaw, a young man seeking revenge for an old injustice, and the abduction of the rancher's daughter. When Jason, the sheriff and Adam meet for the final time, nine men have already died . . .

DOUBLE CROSS TRAIL DRIVE

Chet Cunningham

The journey begins as an ordinary trail drive from Texas to the railroad in Kansas — but soon turns deadly as bullets fly and rustlers try to steal the whole herd of steer . . . Back at the ranch in Texas, the violence continues, as the ranch owner seems to have become a sitting target. Whoever is out to ruin the ranch and kill the owner must be discovered, especially as the final deadly cattle stampede threatens to settle the matter once and for all . . .